RAGE

RAGE

JACKIE MORSE KESSLER

Houghton Mifflin Harcourt
Boston New York 2011

For information about permission to reproduce selections from this book,
write to Permissions, Houghton Mifflin Harcourt Publishing Company,
215 Park Avenue South, New York, New York 10003.

Graphia and the Graphia logo are registered trademarks of
Houghton Mifflin Harcourt Publishing Company.

www.hmhbooks.com

Text set in Adobe Garamond.

Library of Congress Cataloging-in-Publication Data
Kessler, Jackie Morse.
Rage / Jackie Morse Kessler.
p. cm.
Summary: Sixteen-year-old Missy copes with being an outcast at school and stress
at home by cutting herself with a razorblade, until Death chooses her as one of
the Four Horsemen of the Apocalypse, War, and offers her a new blade.
ISBN 978-0-547-44528-1
[1. Cutting (Self-mutilation)—Fiction. 2. Self-mutilation—Fiction. 3. Emotional
problems—Fiction. 4. Family problems—Fiction. 5. Self-acceptance—Fiction. 6. High
schools—Fiction. 7. Schools—Fiction. 8. Four Horsemen of the Apocalypse—Fiction.]
I. Title.
PZ7.K4835Rag 2011
[Fic]—dc22
2010027408

Manufactured in the United States of America
DOM 10 9 8 7 6 5 4 3 2 1
4500284933

If you've ever felt a rolling fury bury you alive,
if you've ever screamed because the words just wouldn't come,
then this one is for you.

ACKNOWLEDGMENTS

It takes a lot of people to make a book. And I'm thankful for all of them.

First, to my incredible agent, Miriam Kriss, who said immediately after *Hunger,* "So which Horseman are you writing about next?"

Next, to my amazing editor, Julie Tibbott, who knows exactly what to do to turn a story into something powerful, and to the entire Houghton Mifflin Harcourt team—from cover art to production to marketing to sales and everything in between, I'm so grateful to you all.

To the Mopey Teenage Bears and the Deadline Dames: World domination, one book at a time!

To Heather Brewer and Renée Barr: You rock, as always!

To Ryan and Mason: You're the best kids a parent could ever ask for. (But you still can't play the Wii on a school night.)

And to my loving husband, Brett: Always. Forever.

||||||

The refugee camp in the desert that Missy visits is based on a real refugee camp.

RAGE

The day Melissa Miller killed her cat, she met the Angel of Death. Except he was no angel—and he wasn't there for the cat. He loomed in the doorway of the Miller house, dappled in sunlight and smiling at Missy as she gaped at him.

"You have blood on your hands," he said.

His words stabbed her, sharp and precise, and her heart jackhammered as if to break free from her chest. "What?"

"Blood," he repeated. "Thick. Red, ranging from maroon to carnelian, depending on the oxygen content. You know," he said cheerfully. "Life."

Don't panic, she told herself. He didn't know. He was just a delivery guy, an anonymous no one in a brown hoodie shirt so long and loose that it blended into his brown cargo pants. A stranger. Even so, sweat popped on Missy's brow as she peered at him. "Who—?"

His smile stretched, cutting off her question as she saw the grin hidden beneath the flesh, all lipless teeth and gallows humor. "You know who I am, Melissa Miller."

And she did.

With that recognition, Missy's knees buckled. Her breath constricted in her throat, trapping her scream.

"So afraid," Death said. His voice wasn't kind, exactly, but it also wasn't cruel; it was the sound of balance, and infinite patience. "And yet, it's fear that's kept you alive. So I won't take it personally."

Her chest tightened, *tightened*, transforming her body into a slow cooker and setting her heart to Boil. She had to cut herself now, right now, bleed out the pain before it swallowed her whole.

But she couldn't move; beneath his hood, Death's stormy gaze had captured her, cemented her feet to the ground.

Missy stammered, "H-How . . . ?" The rest of the question died on her tongue.

He chuckled, the sound like faint music. "You're too adorable. 'What?' 'Who?' 'How?' The 'where,' at least, doesn't need to be asked. And like the others, it really doesn't need to be answered. For thee," he said, motioning.

With that movement, she was able to tear her gaze away from his shadowed face. He was offering her an oblong package: a pristinely, coldly white box. Where the package had come from, Missy couldn't say; it was as if it had always been in his hands and she only now noticed it. Which made no sense, considering that the package was a good three feet long.

Then again, none of this made sense. Death was on her doorstep, bearing a gift like a suitor. *A corsage before the prom,* she thought, and she quashed an insane urge to giggle.

"Take it, Melissa Miller."

Missy reached out with an unsteady hand, slowly, fighting the urge to grab the box. Her fingers ghosted over the package, her nails skimming the white surface and leaving blood-red trails in their wake, trails that quickly faded when she snatched her hand away. She blinked, and the box was once again white and pure, untainted by her touch.

"Why?" she asked, her voice hoarse.

He let out another chuckle, one that slithered up her spine and wrapped around her throat. "Philosophy? Well, then. For you, multiple choice. *A*, why not? *B*, because." He leaned in close and Missy cringed. *"C,"* he said, "you were too overwhelmed to hold your blade precisely. You were going to slice an artery. The spray would have hit you here." He motioned to her eyes, her cheek, her chin. "You would have watched the blood, sitting in stunned silence as your life ebbed, wondering what went wrong and what happened next. It would have looked like suicide," he added, his eyes shining darkly, like starlight trapped in whirlpools. "But you and I both know better. Don't we, Melissa?"

Her head swam with his words, and she squeezed her eyes shut to make the world stop spinning. But darkness was no friend: devoid of sight, she once again heard Graygirl's last pleading meow, warbling and sickly, once again felt the furry body go limp and empty.

"No," she whispered. She opened her eyes, but the darkness remained on her doorstep, grinning at her.

"Yes," said Death. "Take the box, Melissa Miller."

Overwhelmed, she took the box. This time, it remained steadfastly white.

And then Missy slammed the door in Death's face.

She bolted upstairs, the long package tucked under her arm. Voices assaulted her: her father's, from the den, asking who'd been at the door; her mother's, from the upstairs office, chiding her not to slam things.

His voice, dark and velvety soft, intimate and yet cold: *You have blood on your hands.*

Missy ignored them all. Thoughts whirling, she rushed into the safety of her room. She slammed the door (surely earning another reprimand from her mother) and locked it, then dropped the package—barely the size of a flower box now, and shrinking—onto her tattered comforter. The poster on her closet door shimmered in the curtained light. As always, Marilyn Monroe's eyes were closed in ecstasy, and James Dean stared off to the right, his troubled gaze on something Missy couldn't see. By the bottom left of the poster, a red rose was disfigured by the closet doorknob.

She opened the closet door quickly and tucked the white tie box onto the high shelf. She shut the door and finally collapsed on top of her blanket, clutching her pillow to her chest. Her long sleeves chafed her arms; her wrists begged her to strip naked and let the air kiss her skin.

You have blood on your hands.

Her eyes stung. She blinked out the tears, felt them meander down her cheeks, burning saltwater tracks into her flesh. Squeezing her pillow, Missy thought about opening her closet door again—not for the new package, no, but for her lockbox and what was inside of it.

The spray would have hit you here, Death had said. She imagined his fingers caressing her face, wondered if his hands would be cold, like his voice. She almost smiled, but then Death's voice gave way to another, even colder voice.

Freak.

Holding her pillow like a shield, Missy gritted her teeth. No, she couldn't take out the box, no matter how much she wanted to.

With that decision, she forgot about the messenger who'd come to her door, about the white box she'd taken but had not truly accepted.

All she thought now was how she'd show *him* that she wasn't a freak. She didn't need to cut. She could handle it—school, her family, her life, everything. She could do it.

I don't need the blade, she told herself, making it her mantra. *I don't need the blade. I don't.*

Missy bore the first pangs of emotional withdrawal as she imagined the blood vessels that tattooed her body beneath her skin, mapping the way to hidden treasure.

||||||

On the Millers' doorstep, Death stood, mouth agape. The potted plants on either side of the front door sagged, already brown and withered. Overhead, the summer sun winked behind clouds, capricious, turning the sky a picturesque blue, now bleak and on the edge of nightmare, now bright again.

"Well, now," Death eventually said. "That was different."

In the front yard, a pale horse nickered.

Death shook his head as he approached his steed. "I didn't even charge her with her task. Slammed the door in my face. In my *face*." He chuckled. "I don't know if I'm insulted or amused."

The pale horse snorted.

"You're right," he said, patting his steed's powerful neck. "Definitely amused. I like her."

The horse blinked, perhaps reproachfully.

"Can I help it if I have a type?"

This time, the horse didn't answer.

Death climbed up in a practiced motion, limbs fluid and graceful. Once again the Pale Rider of the Apocalypse, he said, "Let's move on. That car crash over on Third isn't going to unsmash itself."

The steed's ears twitched toward the Miller house, and the horse blew out a question in the way that horses do.

"Her? Not a problem." Death smiled warmly. "I can wait."

FRIDAY

CHAPTER 1

If Melissa Miller were an artist, she would have painted the world in vicious streaks of red. Nothing like Picasso's rose period, all soft and cheerful and so optimistic that it made you want to puke. Missy's red phase would have been brutal and bright enough to cut your eyes. Missy's art would have been honest.

She gripped the charcoal stick like a weapon, stroking it cleanly across the paper.

"Negative space," Ms. Helfand said as Missy worked. "It's negative space and you're just filling in what's already there."

Yeah. Whatever. Missy sliced, and the paper bled charcoal.

Seated across from her, Erica whispered, "You going to Kevin's tonight?"

Missy shrugged, one shouldered, the epitome of Couldn't Care Less. She kept sketching, filling the white paper with streaks of black.

"Yeah," Erica agreed. "I don't know, either." She was aiming for indifferent and missed by a mile. Ever since sophomore year, Erica had been one of those types who care about what people think of them. She was someone who needed to be where the crowd was going.

Missy was not. Missy was the stone in the sea; Erica was driftwood caught in the tide. Most of the junior class (and a good chunk of seniors) would be at Kevin's party tonight, so of course Erica was going, no matter what she was saying now.

Weak.

Missy took the thought and stuffed it down into the glass jar of her heart, sealing the lid with a blink. Her face remained impassive as she forced her emotions into submission—no pull of her mouth, no squint of her eyes, nothing to betray any hint of exasperation or anger. It was her day face, her dead face, the one she painted every morning before leaving the safety of her bedroom. It helped her blend with all the normal people.

"Could be fun," Erica said gamely.

"Or a waste of time," Missy replied, bored.

"I guess." Erica might have said more, but Ms. Helfand's heels clacked on the linoleum floor, so the girl bent her head to her work. From what Missy glimpsed, Erica was drawing roadkill.

The teacher stopped two tables away, but Missy didn't take that as a cue to continue the conversation. Lately, she didn't talk if it wasn't necessary, not even to Erica, who used to be someone Missy called a friend. Much better to keep everything inside, down in the dark where people never saw or heard the truth. In the dark, you couldn't see when you were bleeding.

Relishing the silence, Missy sketched. Shadows slowly filled her paper, spreading like cancer from each of the corners. In its center, the unfilled part suggested the shape of a lowercase *t*.

"You used to like going out," Erica said softly.

Missy darted a glance at the other girl. Erica was chewing her bottom lip and staring intently at her own picture. It was almost as if she was afraid to look at Missy.

If the notion bothered Missy, it was eclipsed by the more pressing thought: *She doesn't get it.* Wrapped around the charcoal stick, Missy's knuckles whitened. No one got it. No one understood. Not Erica. Not Missy's folks. Not her sister.

Not Adam.

God, no, Adam hadn't understood, no matter how many times he'd told her he loved her, how he'd made such incredible promises and, far worse, made her believe those promises . . .

In her mind, a word whispered like the hiss of oil on a skillet: *Freak.*

Missy shoved the thoughts and feelings down into their prison of the glass jar. Only once the lid was sealed tight did she release her breath. She glanced over at Erica to see if she had noticed her brief internal struggle. She shouldn't have worried. Erica sat slumped, oblivious, halfheartedly moving her charcoal stick across her paper.

Maybe Erica didn't understand her anymore. But that didn't mean Missy had to be a complete turd about it. So she threw the other girl a bone. "Maybe I'll go."

The look of gratitude on Erica's face made Missy slightly nauseated. When had they ever had anything in common? Had Missy really been that desperate?

Erica grinned hugely. "What'll you wear?"

"The usual." Translation: *Black and black and black, duh.*

Erica tittered laughter, muffled quickly by her hand. "Me too."

Of course. Missy wore black because it was the color of her soul. Erica wore black because it was trendy.

"I'm so glad you're going," Erica said, gushing. "It's going to be awesome. You'll see. Kevin does the best parties. Remember last year?"

Of course Missy did: she'd hooked up with Adam during that party. They'd left in Adam's parents' car long before the police arrived to break things up. And she'd left her virginity in the back seat.

No. No no no. Don't think about him.

Before she could correct Erica—Missy had never said she would go to Kevin's party, only that she might—Ms. Helfand approached their table. She leaned over Missy, all expensive perfume that didn't mask the need for better deodorant, and she made appreciative noises as she looked at Missy's picture.

"Excellent use of negative space," Ms. Helfand cooed. "Bold strokes, showing a confident hand. And the white crucifix is an excellent contrast to the darkness surrounding it. I especially like how the cross is not upright. It suggests a struggle, even with it bathed in light. Marvelous work, Melissa. Very spiritual."

Missy might have blushed, but the dead face obscured it. She murmured her thanks. She knew that art was best left to interpretation, so she didn't correct Ms. Helfand. Missy hadn't drawn a crucifix.

On her paper, the white sword gleamed.

||||||

Between classes: the time when high school morphs into a no man's land of cliques and wannabes. Either you choose a side or you get caught in a volley of rapid fire and go down hard, your reputation slaughtered.

Missy was used to the open warfare of high school. She sidestepped the carnage of snubbing by plowing forward, indifferent to the catcalls and pointed looks thrown her way. So what if people called her a poser, a loser, a goth? It didn't matter. None of it mattered. She marched, ignoring the clandestine texting that took place around the students' social battles. Less than four minutes to get to fourth-period world history—Missy didn't have time to be sidetracked by idiots.

And yet, there by the lockers was Adam and his crew, Adam with a smirk on those full lips, his eyes daring her to stop and talk to him, to react to him. Missy walked on, eyes straight ahead, clutching her binder and books to her chest.

"Freak alert," crowed one of the guys—either Matt 1 or Matt 2, one of Adam's bro-hos, his adoring fans who thought he was God. Missy could never keep the Matts straight, even when she and Adam had been together.

"Emo cutter girl," said the other Matt. "Careful—she'll bleed all over you."

"Or cry all over you."

"Cries as she bleeds. Where you going, emo cutter girl?"

Her dead face stayed on, mouth sealed, gaze set to Screw You. *Words,* she told herself. They were just words. And never mind that they were true words.

She ignored Matt 1 and Matt 2 and the other guys standing there with Adam as she went to her locker to swap out her morning textbooks for her afternoon load. The Matts kept insulting her, calling her "emo dyke" (which was just stupid, because she'd never been into girls) and "cutterslut" and even "dead prude walking." She came close to rolling her eyes. How could she be a slut *and* a prude? Bad enough she was being taunted by jerks. Couldn't she at least be taunted by jerks who understood the words they said?

Worse, though, was part of her held her breath, waiting to see what Adam would do.

She dumped her books in her locker, silently chiding herself for thinking about Adam at all. So what that they'd been together for nine months and twenty-eight days? So what that he'd been her first? *Adam + Missy* had ended more than two months ago. Their relationship was past tense. Pluperfect, even. They were done, finished, stick-a-fork-in-me, pencils-down done.

And then she heard his voice, clear as birdsong on a spring morning: "Looking hot under all the black."

No. No *way* was he hitting on her.

Like a switch had been flipped, the Matts changed their taunts to comment on her looks, and now some of the other boys in the group joined in. But Missy barely heard them over her pounding heart. Why was Adam hitting on her? She stole a glance from the cautious barrier of her overlong bangs—and yes, he was looking at her, looking *into* her, his eyes burning a hole in her heart. Her stomach clenched, and in a sudden flash of tactile memory she could feel his hands on her, doing such things to her . . .

She grabbed her afternoon pile of books and slammed her locker, then quickly fumbled on the combination lock.

"Be seeing you," Adam said.

Not if she could help it. Missy fled down the hall, her ears ringing with the Matts' laughter, her stupid body reminding her just how much she missed being with Adam. And that slowly turned to panic. The familiar feeling of suffocation leeched its way through her, making each breath torture, and her heart screamed behind the prison of her ribs.

She thought desperately of her lockbox, tucked safely away in her closet.

Not again, she told herself. *Not again.*

Whether she meant Adam or her razorblade, Missy couldn't say.

||||||

As soon as Missy vanished around the corner, Adam turned to the others. "Grabbing a smoke," he announced, and the other boys all got in line, like soldiers. Or lemmings.

"Rah, carcinogens," said Death. Of course, the boys didn't hear him. They were in the prime of life, and because they weren't chosen to be Horsemen, there was no reason they should notice Death at all.

Give it about twenty years with their pack-a-day habit. Then they'd notice him, all right.

Death could have followed Missy, but he didn't bother. She didn't know it, but tonight was going to be a big night for her. And if Death wanted to be there, he'd better get his work done for the day. Being the epitome of patience wasn't an excuse to be a slacker.

Whistling a jaunty tune, he sauntered out of the school.

CHAPTER 2

Missy dove. She hit the ground hard on her side, her shoulder taking the brunt of the impact. But she didn't feel the sting; she was too busy cradling the soccer ball to her gut.

"Nice one!" Bella pumped her fist in the air. "Now up! Six seconds! Go!"

Missy scrambled to her feet and pivoted right, throwing the ball two-handed over her head. Bella, though, had anticipated the direction correctly and was already body-blocking the shot, and now she was dribbling the ball, backing up for another attempt on the goal.

"Got to use your body better," she scolded, dancing backward. "You practically texted the direction. Fakeout. Just because you're a goalie doesn't mean you can't be shrewd."

Breathing heavily, Missy dropped into a low ready position, pretending she didn't feel the burn in her thighs. The rich smells of grass and dirt tickled her nostrils, and beneath that was the familiar odor of hard-earned sweat. She blinked perspiration out of her eyes, telling herself yet again that she needed a sweatband on her forehead. She swayed left, then right, her gaze locked on the soccer ball.

"You taking a nap?" Bella laughed. "Don't just squat there in the goal box! Come out and grab the ball! I dare you!"

Missy didn't take the bait. If she darted forward, she'd be committed to that and would have to block the shot while leaving the goal unprotected. Bella arced left, and Missy shuffled right, galloping sideways.

"It's not enough to watch the ball," Bella said, moving right, now left again, coming forward and then darting to the side. "Watch my hips. But always follow the ball. Don't look away too long, because the ball moves fast." She emphasized the point with a powerhouse kick, aimed high.

Eyes on the ball, Missy lifted her right knee and pushed off with her left leg, reaching long. Thumbs together so that her hands made a *W,* she caught the ball and rode it to the ground.

"Good! Six seconds. Go!"

Again, Missy hurled the ball away—and this time it got some distance before Bella got it under control. Missy took a moment to palm sweaty hair off her forehead and glance at the rest of the team. The girls, paired off, were scattered across the field, some doing passing drills, others attempting scoring shots while the partner tried to block or steal as the coach called out pointers. It was a good team this year, but they'd lose a boatload of seniors after graduation. Like Bella. But that meant that next year Missy would be the primary goalkeeper and one of the JV girls would be where Missy was now: drilling like mad for the time when she'd be the last line of defense.

The protector.

The thought made Missy grin. Here she didn't need her dead face. Here she didn't hide her heart in a glass jar and pray to God or whoever that it would never break again. Here it didn't matter that she was a freak, a loser, just a girl sailing through what passed as life.

Here, on the battlefield, Missy was home.

Bathed in sweat and adrenaline, Missy spread her arms wide

and barked out a laugh—a raw sound, a primal sound, one that evoked joy and bloodshed in equal parts. It was the sound of jubilant violence.

But here was Bella again, approaching on a zigzag. Missy turned to face her opponent, and she caught a panoramic sweep of the people speckling the bleachers—some girls, a few guys who got their kicks watching girls get sweaty, a parent or two who'd taken "soccer mom" to the extreme by coming to the practices. And there, standing on the sidelines near the locker room, was a woman in black—as black as a dead heart, from her wide-brimmed hat to her trench coat to her boots—just standing there, watching the players.

No. Watching *Missy.*

"Heads!"

Missy spun just as the ball slammed into her stomach. She doubled over and went down hard. Even as she lay on her back, breathless, she saw the black-garbed woman, as if a flashbulb had burned her image on Missy's retinas.

Black as death, she thought, and on the heels of that: *She's not Death.*

As if *that* made any sense.

Bella ran over to help her up. "Christ, Missy, you okay?"

Biting her lip, Missy nodded.

"Good." Then Bella slapped her upside the head. "The hell were you doing, staring off into space? Come on, girl. You know better. You want to be goalie, you got to keep your head in the game."

"Sorry," Missy muttered, hands clasped on her stomach. "Saw someone . . ." Her voice trailed off as she stared by the locker room door, where no one stood in black, let alone at all. The woman had disappeared.

"Someone what? Coming at you?" Bella scanned the field as if to see who was ignoring the coach's orders to pair off.

"No. It was nothing. Just got distracted." Missy's stomach hurt, but that, too, was a distraction. Soccer means getting hurt. You have to have a high pain tolerance to play, especially if you're goalie. You're going to get kicked, and not always politely on the shin guard. You're going to have balls zooming at you, ready to take your head off. And you have to get in the way of the shot, even knowing that it's going to hurt.

Pain never stopped Missy. Truth be told, she relished it. On the soccer field, she was more alive than anywhere else. It was the one place where she could be herself, feel things the way she was meant to feel them—without getting overwhelmed, without it being like a hand squeezing her heart or gripping her throat.

When she played soccer, Missy could finally breathe freely after a day of slow suffocation.

"All right," Bella said, clapping Missy's shoulder. "Stretch out with me."

She led Missy through the exercises, pummeling Missy with words of wisdom as she did so.

"Even if someone's coming at you, you can't freeze," Bella said, bending over one leg. "Don't be afraid. Be confident. Don't be scared and run away from the ball. I promise you, there are things a lot scarier than soccer balls. Like the boys' locker room. Be confident. Block the shot."

Missy absorbed the advice like blows to the body.

"You don't even have to touch the ball," Bella said. "Intimidate the hell out of your opponent. Scare your opponent into missing the shot. You don't have to block what doesn't come near the goal."

"Isn't it better to make the save?"

"Making a killer save feels great, but if you make them screw up the shot, or if you organize the defense well enough that they can't take a shot at all, you've done your job. Think outside of the goal box."

Missy grinned at the lame joke because she knew Bella expected it, and then she looked once more toward the locker room. The woman in black was gone—if she'd ever been there at all.

||||||

Missy took her time in the locker room, first stripping off the gloves and cleats and soccer socks and shin guards, then going into the bathroom to change her clothes. Unlike the others, she wasn't in a rush to get home—she'd taken care of her homework during her study period, and despite what Erica thought, she wasn't going to Kevin's stupid party, where stupid Adam and his stupid friends would definitely be.

Looking hot under all the black.

She squeezed her nails into her palms, squeezed until her hands wept. The last thing she wanted to be thinking about was Adam, but there she was, alone in the girls' locker room, remembering what it was like for his hands to travel over her body, the feeling of his mouth on hers . . . remembering his husky declarations of love even as he fumbled with her zipper.

Missy closed her eyes and took a shuddering breath, then shoved the memory down down down into the glass jar. Only after she'd sealed the lid again did she open her eyes. If she tried, she could pretend the tears were just sweat.

Maybe she should take out her lockbox tonight.

No, she thought, and *No* again. Aloud she whispered, "I don't need the blade."

A kiss of wind, like frost on the nape of her neck.

"I don't," she said again, insistent. Unclenching her fingers, she watched the half-moon imprints fill with blood. *Tiny mouths,* she thought, staring at the maroon slices. *Tiny mouths waiting to be fed . . .*

Her stomach growled, like a warning, and she realized she was hungry. Starving.

Missy grabbed her water bottle and drained it. Shaking out the last drops into her mouth, she berated herself for not having at least a granola bar with her. When she got home, she was going to raid the fridge, and never mind that dinner would be in an hour.

A hint of shadow caught her eye, darker than dark, over by the back wall. It almost looked like the outline of a person, a silhouette in a spill of black ink. Missy frowned as she stared at the shadow, thinking how odd the lighting was and that of course she was alone, she'd said her goodbyes to everyone else . . .

And then her phone vibrated, announcing a text message. Missy tore her gaze from the dark spot and pulled her cell phone from her pocket. She glanced at the screen.

Adam.

She sat down hard on the bench. *Why?* she thought, despairing. She knew she should delete it without reading it, knew it would be the textbook definition of *mistake* if she read his message.

Her lips tingled as she remembered the feeling of his mouth on hers, and she suddenly hungered for him, missed him so completely that it was a physical ache. She checked the message.

C U @ KEVS 2NITE?

The world whited out in a blinding moment of utter panic. Her heart slammed in her chest, galloping, rocketing now, threatening to go nuclear. Sweat popped on her brow, and her stomach knotted viciously.

. . . no no no no no . . .

Her blade. She needed her blade. She needed to bleed out the badness, needed the blood to breathe again.

Her hands shook, and the phone slipped between her numb fingers. It hit the bare floor, clattering. The sound snapped Missy out of her anxiety attack. She scooped up her phone and checked to make sure it still worked. Damn it, if Adam made her break her phone, she'd kill him.

She almost heard Bella's voice reprimanding her: *Don't blame the defense if you miss a block and the other team gets the goal.*

Missy gritted her teeth. She'd been the one who'd dropped the phone. Not Adam. Luckily, the phone still worked, so she didn't have to worry about where to place the blame. Blood pounded in her ears as she reread Adam's text. Before she could rethink it, her thumbs moved, flowing over the keyboard with practiced ease. She replied:

WHY?

She sat, holding her breath as she waited for his response. *Stupid,* she told herself, *stupid stupid stupid* . . .

The phone vibrated, and she checked the new message.

B/C I MISS U

Oh God.

It was a joke. A prank. The Matts put him up to it. He just wanted to screw with her—or maybe just screw her, use her and dump her like Kleenex. Her head felt too light, and it was impossible for her to take a deep breath.

Another text from him:

C U 2NITE?

Hating herself, she replied:

MAYBE

And then she turned off her cell phone.

For a long moment, Missy just sat in the dim locker room, feeling her heartbeat thump through her body, hearing the sounds of her own ragged breathing. Then she grabbed her things, stuffed everything into her duffle bag, and shoved her

feet into her boots. She had to race home and shower and figure out what the hell to wear to Kevin's.

IIIII

The woman dressed in black from head to foot stepped away
from the shadows and watched the girl zoom out of the locker
room. Once the door slammed shut, the woman smiled, a
thing of teeth and appetite.

"From the way he talks about her," Famine said aloud,
"you'd think she was taller."

CHAPTER 3

Missy got home just before 6:30, smack dab in the middle of dinner prep. So at 6:34, after she'd kicked her boots off in the mudroom and washed her hands, Missy was chopping vegetables on the kitchen island while Sue was garlicking up the loaf of Italian bread. Their mom bustled between the kitchen and the dining room, grabbing plates and utensils and dropping helpful comments about how Susan should be sure to layer both sides and Melissa should hold the knife just so. As if Missy needed any help with that.

After their mom hightailed it back into the dining room, Sue muttered, "God, reek much?"

Dead face firmly in place, Missy said nothing as she chopped.

"I forgot," Sue trilled. "Emos don't shower. They just bathe in their own tears."

Missy asked, "Hear that?" She paused, listening, then said, "That's the sound of me not giving a damn what you think."

Sue rolled her eyes. "You are *such* a loser. Bet you want to grow up to be a vampire."

Missy thought of how much she'd love to bash Sue's teeth in, and never mind that she'd scrape her knuckles on the hidden braces. Sue didn't know the first thing about Missy. No one did. "I'm sorry," Missy said, "I don't speak poser."

"No, but you're fluent in asshat."

The girls glared at each other so heatedly, it was a minor miracle the air between them didn't catch fire.

"Susan," their mom called, "help me with this, would you?"

Sue's hateful look melted into the classic Mom-loves-me-best smirk before she sashayed to the dining room.

Missy stuck her tongue out at Sue's back and thought very dark thoughts about her little sister. Only a freshman but already a grade-A bitch: that was Susan Miller. Sure, there'd been a time when Missy and Sue had been the best of friends. But that had been a lifetime ago. Once Sue hit high school, she'd morphed into Teen Barbie, complete with the plastic veneer: cheer squad, debate team, student council, a string of boyfriends in her wake. The day Sue had realized that her crowd made it their business to insult people who looked and acted like Missy had been the day the siblings' friendship ended. At first, Missy had watched Sue's descent into popularity and wondered how anyone could be so perpetually *on* and not lose themselves. Then the daily taunts had started in earnest and Missy had stopped caring about her sister at all.

She really didn't give a damn what her sister thought of her. Lips pressed together tightly, Missy diced a cucumber. Sue could just drop dead.

It would have looked like suicide, a cold voice whispered.

Missy almost jumped out of her skin. She whirled around, knife in hand—but no one was there. Sue was kissing up to their mom in the other room, and their dad hadn't come home yet.

Missy was alone.

Clearly, she was losing her mind. If she really were emo, like Sue and everyone thought, she'd write a poem about it.

Letting out a shaky laugh, Missy started chopping the cucumber again. She was just stressed out over going to the party; that was all. She glanced at the time on the oven clock and bit her lip. At this rate, she'd never be ready by 8:30.

The thought froze her, and then she berated herself for caring about the time. She'd show up at Kevin's when she was good and ready, and not a moment sooner. If she didn't see Adam there, it was no big deal.

And if he did get there before her, well, he could just wait.

Smiling grimly, she chopped with more vigor.

Her father walked through the door at 6:50, and dinner was served at 7:00. Dinnertime in the Miller household was family time, as Mr. and Mrs. Miller had always insisted, so as they passed around the plate of garlic bread and scooped out the spaghetti, they went around the table, talking about their day. Dad was all about the upcoming office launch, as usual, talking about network systems and T1 lines and whatnot and how the CEO kept changing his expectations so Dad had to keep changing the specs. Mom chatted about how the marketing chief and the Internet marketing director wanted Mom and her team to meet with them next week to discuss a microsite for the company's business journal. Missy listened with feigned interest, asking pointed questions at the right moments to prove that she was really listening and, more than that, really cared.

As Sue prattled about her latest boyfriend and her latest cheer routine, Missy slurped on spaghetti, chewing every bite thirty times before swallowing. Silently counting the bites let her mostly tune out her sister's nails-on-a-blackboard voice.

When Missy's turn arrived, she shrugged and said, "Got an A on my chem test. Had soccer practice. Going to start in tomorrow's game. Going to a party tonight."

The table erupted in chatter—Dad was thrilled about Missy finally getting her chance to shine as goalkeeper; Mom was ecstatic over the A in chemistry and all "See how the studying pays off?" Sue silently fumed, but whether that was over the attention Missy was getting or over the tidbit that Missy was going to Kevin's party was impossible to say. Both girls had an understanding: hating each other was fine, but not in front of the parents. Sue probably just didn't want to blow her image as a perfect daughter. Missy didn't want their parents involved—knowing them, they'd try to mediate by locking Missy and Sue into the bathroom until they worked out their differences.

But after a few minutes of their parents gushing over Missy, an ugly smile bloomed on Sue's face, poisonously sweet. "Hey, Mom, Dad? Could we get a new cat?"

Missy's heart stopped.

"I really miss Graygirl," Sue said, half petulance, half pleading.

Missy felt the blood drain from her face as she heard Graygirl's final cry, and once again she was holding the cat's dead body, felt it when the spark that had made Graygirl *Graygirl* fade to nothing and all that was left was a shell covered in old fur.

"The house does feel empty without a cat," her mom said. And her dad was nodding his head, saying that maybe they could get a couple of kittens, one for each of the girls.

You have blood on your hands.

Oh, God.

Missy had to leave, right now. "Excuse me," she said thickly as she scraped back her chair. "I have to go shower."

"Melissa, you barely ate," her mother chided.

"Lost my appetite." Missy tossed her fork and napkin onto her mostly full plate, grabbed the dish and her water glass, and tromped into the kitchen. She dumped the food into the garbage and left the dinnerware in the sink. Somehow, she managed not to vomit.

The spray would have hit you here.

She bolted up the stairs and dashed into the bathroom, slamming the door behind her. Over the machine-gun fire of her heartbeat, she heard her mom call out something about slamming doors.

Missy was losing her mind. No other explanation for it. Hearing voices, remembering something that never happened— definitely insane. Probably certifiable.

She turned on the shower and began stripping off her clothes: First the long-sleeved black hoodie and then the ripped black denim shorts, yanking them off so quickly that she scored another run in her red and black striped tights. Next the black sports bra—a must during soccer days—and finally her panties, bright red. Let people think she didn't wear anything that didn't have black on it. She knew better.

Waiting for the water to heat, she ran her hands over her biceps, the pads of her fingers dancing along the raised scars. Her hands flowed over the thin lines on her shoulders, then down, over her wounded belly, her gouged inner thighs, then back up, as all the while she kept her gaze on the water.

The house does feel empty without a cat.

Swallowing her sob, Missy stepped into the shower and stood gasping under the scorching spray. She soaped and rinsed and lathered and rinsed and conditioned, all with the mindlessness of everyday routine. Then she coated her legs with shaving gel and took her oh-so-girly pink disposable razor and began to shave, running the cheap blade from ankle to knee, from knee to groin, slowly, almost lovingly. First legs, then bikini area, and last her armpits, all without a knick or scrape. When she finished, she held out her hands in penance, letting the steaming water absolve her of her sins.

Back in her room, now clean and toweled dry, she stood in her full-length bathrobe, staring at the spot on her bed where Graygirl had always been. If Missy turned, she knew she'd still see the cat sprawled in her usual place near the footboard, eyes closed and mouth pulled in a secretive feline smile, purring her contentment.

At the end, all she'd been was flesh and bones.

Blinking away sudden tears, Missy tore through her closet. Tops and skirts and pants, all imperfect and wrong. She had nothing to wear. Her clothing was flawed.

Her life was flawed.

She sank to her knees, hugging herself tightly. Buried at the bottom of her closet, her lockbox beckoned with promises of razor-sharp kisses, whispering that she could bleed out the badness.

Then his voice, Adam's voice, condemning her and branding her: *Freak.*

She rocked, gripping her elbows and worrying her bottom lip between her teeth. *I don't need the blade,* she told herself. *I don't. Please, God. I don't.*

||||||

Sequestered on the top shelf of the closet, a white tie box waited patiently.

||||||

Outside the Miller house, a pale horse and a black horse stood side by side, eating the grass. The black horse ate as if starving, and the pale horse ate to pass the time. Beneath their hooves, the lawn withered, parched and dying.

The Black Rider listened as Death sang and played his guitar, his long fingers moving easily over the instrument's neck. The music was soothing to Famine; it was a reminder of her previous life, which she'd so recently given up to wield the Scales. Though she was one to school her reactions quite carefully—all things must be measured and treasured, after all, and emotions were no exception—she allowed herself to enjoy the moment.

When the last notes faded into the evening, she said, "It's almost as if you're human."

Death winked at her. "Almost. Come to see if your influence had its desired effect?"

If she blushed, it was hidden beneath the shadow of her wide-brimmed hat. "Some of us aren't as patient as you."

"No one is as patient as me."

Famine saw the truth in that.

"You know," Death said, "the two previous Black Riders didn't get along with the Red."

She sniffed her disdain. "Probably because the previous War slaughtered one Famine and tried to do so to the other."

"Probably," Death agreed cheerfully. "It makes one wonder why you're so eager to see the Red seat filled once more."

Famine frowned at Death, and for a time she said nothing. Eventually she replied, "We need balance."

"Ah." A slow grin played over his face. "You do have an intimate understanding of the importance of balance, don't you?"

She, too, smiled—but hers was a quick thing, as if the notion of humor was fleeting. "You taught me well."

"Such flattery. One would think you want something."

In for a penny and all that. "Will you tell me if we must wait much longer?"

Death strummed a D chord thoughtfully before replying. "'All it takes is one bad day to reduce the sanest man alive to lunacy.'"

The Black Rider arched a slender brow. "Nietzsche?"

"Moore." He strummed an A chord, followed by a G and another D. "Our girl's about to have a very bad day." With that, he began to play a song, and he lent his voice to the music.

Famine looked to the sky, but unlike the song, there was no bad moon rising—there was no moonlight at all tonight. Even so, Death's message was clear.

The girl would make her choice tonight.

The Black Rider nodded. As far as Red candidates went, the girl wasn't *that* bad. Maybe she'd make a good War.

And if not, Famine would just have to destroy her again.

CHAPTER 4

Missy heard the party from halfway down the block. She figured it would be about two hours before the neighbors finally decided enough was enough and called the cops.

Plenty of time for her to go in, make the rounds, and get out. And if she didn't see Adam, so what? She could still tell him that she'd been there and too bad, so sad, guess he just didn't see her.

She gritted her teeth. No, she wouldn't tell him a damn thing. She wasn't talking to him. Wasn't texting him. Wasn't anything with him, ever again. She was nothing but a freak to him.

Looking hot under all the black.

Missy shuddered. Rubbing her arms did nothing to stop the chill, so she let the shudder take her, move through her until it passed. Its touch left her frozen inside, a bone-deep cold that iced over the glass jar of her heart.

She nodded grimly to herself. Much better.

As she walked the rest of the way to Kevin's house, Missy cemented her dead face until even thoughts of Adam couldn't crack it. She was girded for war: Her hair in its gelled points was set to Sharp; her makeup, from eyeliner to lipliner, was masklike perfection. Her outfit was black on black, slashed with red and bruised with indigo. Her velvet boots hinted at softness, which was belied by the gleaming silver buckles and stiletto heels.

Melissa Miller was untouchable.

She approached, weaving her way around a spill of people outside Kevin's house. They dotted the lawn like aphids, feeding on gossip, decimating reputations in their hunger for destruction. Posers, every single one of them. If any deigned to notice Missy, she ignored them. She was on a mission: Get in, get out. As long as she was seen, her job was done. The sounds of music and conversation drowned out the frantic beating of her heart.

She wasn't nervous, she told herself as she worked her way toward the front door. There was nothing to be nervous about. In and out. Done. A comment from Random Poser about how emos thought you cut the grass with razorblades ricocheted off her without a flinch.

She was marble; she was granite. Missy pushed forward.

The open door was barricaded by a huddle of jocks on the front stoop, all clutching plastic cups and talking too loudly, presumably to be heard over the pounding of music from inside the house. One of the Matts leered at her as she squeezed past. "Cutterslut's here," he said, his breath fetid with booze and hormones. The other jocks jeered, insulting her looks and intelligence even as she felt a hand slide over her ass.

She was ice. She was the queen of winter. Their opinions and groping hands meant nothing.

Once inside, her senses slammed into overload. Music first and foremost, stabbing her, vibrating along her teeth and threatening to pop an eardrum. Alcohol and sweat next, stinging her nostrils. And the people—everywhere she looked, teenagers were gathered, dancing and talking, drinking and scoping, making out in the corners and casting heated glances over shoulders. The air was thick with intention. It wasn't a party as much as it was a meat market. But then, no one really expected anything else. Going to parties junior year wasn't so much about having a social life as it was about progressing your love life.

Or about showing your ex just how fine you were without him.

Missy did a slow circuit, eyeballing groups as she sauntered by. There was Erica, clinging to another girl who looked just as desperate as Erica did: too wide-eyed, smiles too big, practically begging anyone and everyone to please come talk to them. Over by the stereo was Kevin himself, surrounded by a wall of hangers-on and wannabes. A few of the varsity soccer girls breezed past, nodding their hellos to Missy. She turned, opening her mouth to ask one of them (Jenny or Jenna or just Jen; the girl changed nicknames the way most people changed their underwear) where she got her fabulous shredded skirt, but by the time the words were on Missy's tongue, the girls were long gone.

She closed her mouth, setting it in a tight smile. Then she walked over to Erica, who looked like Missy had just saved her life. Erica showered Missy in gratitude, mostly in the form of poor attempts at scathing social commentary. Erica didn't have either the natural bitchiness or the learned comedic timing to make her snark do anything but backfire. Missy limited herself to monosyllabic replies. Neither Erica nor her equally insipid friend noticed Missy's lack of interest.

After a few agonizing minutes of strained conversation, Missy excused herself to get something to drink. Slowly—because God, the place was just that packed—she worked her way to the kitchen, which was even more infested with people than the living room. Of course; the booze was here. She avoided the over-size punchbowl, brimming with drunken orange slices gleaming wetly in a sea of artificial red. Scanning the cola choices, she grabbed a can of Cherry Coke and popped the top.

His voice, low and lush, by her ear: "Hey, you *did* show."

Missy took a slow, deliberate sip of cola before she turned to face Adam. He was looking lickably good, damn him, and from the sparkle in his eye, he knew it. Missy shrugged as if bored. "Decided to check it out."

"Because I'm here?"

"You wish."

He leaned in close. Missy smelled his cologne and, beneath that, a hint of sweat. It was a heady combination, something purely masculine that made her hormones sing, and she forced herself not to close her eyes and just breathe him in.

Adam said, "Maybe I do wish."

In its frozen prison, her heart thumped harder. He was lying. He had to be lying. She smiled, knowing he saw only her dead face and that he couldn't see, couldn't know, how a part of her still wished that he wasn't lying at all. "Maybe you're full of crap."

He clutched a hand to his chest. "Ouch," he said, winking.

Missy took in that wink, that knowing smile on his face, and all she could think was *He's a user he's a poser he called you a freak and told his friends about your scars.* She allowed herself a tiny smile—a dead smile, nothing more than a twitch of her lips. "If *that* hurt," she said sweetly, "I don't know how you get through football practice without running home crying to your mommy."

With those words, she pushed past him and left the kitchen.

She was floating, soaring. She'd spoken to Adam and hadn't died or melted or exploded. She hadn't made an idiot of herself. She'd held her own, and in public. She wanted to pump her fist in the air and cheer. Sipping her drink, Missy sauntered like a runway model, full of swagger, radiating confidence that bordered on smugness.

"Hey," Erica said as Missy rejoined her. "No punch?"

"Not in the mood for booze," Missy said. Which was true: alcohol might make her do or say something stupid, and with Adam and so many of his posse here, Missy couldn't take that chance. She drank a little more. When she was done with her soda, she'd leave. God knew, she didn't want to stay at the stupid party. She—

"Missy," Adam said *right behind her,* "you just left me hanging."

She stiffened. This wasn't supposed to happen. She'd shot him down; he was supposed to crawl back to his friends and leave her the hell alone, her pride intact. Without turning around, she said to Erica, "Do you hear something?"

But Erica didn't know how to play that game. "Adam just said you left him hanging."

Missy thought very, very black thoughts—about Erica, about Adam, about the world in general. She turned, slowly, her gaze all but shrieking *Drop Dead.* Adam was right there, looking gorgeous, waiting for her response. Blood pounded in her ears, behind her eyes; with every heartbeat, anger surged. But along with the anger was a whisper of dismay. Why wouldn't he just leave her alone? They were pushing-up-daisies done.

Unless maybe he didn't want them to be done.

No, *no.* He was playing with her. She demanded, "What do you want?"

He opened his mouth, then seemed to reconsider his response, because he shoved his hands in his pockets and smiled sheepishly. He said, "I miss you."

Oh God.

Over the wild pounding of her heart, she said through gritted teeth, "You dumped me, called me names." Even now, she heard him whisper *freak,* but that was only in her mind. Adam himself was right here, right in front of her and looking at her in that way of his, making her skin tingle.

"I was a dick. I'm sorry," he said, reaching over to touch her face, once, lightly stroking her cheek before darting his hand away.

Where he'd touched her, she was on fire. That heat melted the ice around the glass jar of her heart, set her blood to Simmer. She swallowed thickly, not trusting him, wanting more than anything to trust him. She said, "Two months too late."

"Let me make it up to you."

"How're you going to do that?"

"Like this." And then he was holding her close, and she was staring up into his eyes. For a shining moment, she thought clearly, *This is a bad idea.* But then he was kissing her, and Missy stopped thinking at all.

||||||

"I'll kiss your open sores," Death sang—a quiet threat, an insidious promise.

Famine shuddered, overwhelmed. It wasn't just the way Death played the guitar, or the passion in his voice, or even the lyrics themselves, but rather a combination of all three—the words, the music, his passion, all blending seamlessly into something that hooked into the Black Rider's heart and left her bleeding.

Death played on, and Famine shivered.

||||||

Missy didn't know if they were in Kevin's bedroom or his brother's, and it didn't matter. It was a room with a bed, and a door to seal them away from the rest of the world.

The moment Adam had kissed her, her dead face splintered. When she'd kissed him back, her dead face cracked open wide. And by the time they were upstairs, all hands and mouths and tongues, her dead face had slipped off, long forgotten. Even with her clothing on, Missy was naked before him. And she didn't notice.

They kissed and kissed and more than kissed, there in the dimly lit bedroom. Intoxicated by his touches, Missy wondered how she ever could have thought she was the queen of winter. She was flushed, heated from within, and her heart was broiling in her chest. She was liquid fire.

"Take off your clothes," Adam whispered, his hands doing things that made Missy's head spin.

She kicked off her boots and tugged down her skirt. She unrolled her stockings, forcing herself to go slow, silently grateful she'd worn the sexy panties.

"More," he said, his hands sliding up her bare legs.

Breathing hard, she pulled off her top.

Adam took a moment to appreciate her bra and what was within the bra. "Everything off," he murmured. "I want to see you. Really see you."

She fumbled with her bra clasp, her fingers slipping because she was nervous and horny and couldn't stop to think. All there was to the world was Adam and Missy, his hands on her body, his mouth on her skin.

She dropped her bra onto the floor.

"Everything," he rasped.

Panting, she shucked off her underwear.

Adam kissed her once more, deeply, then stepped backward, his heated gaze roaming over her body. She stood before him, stripped, her scars revealed. She had a moment of worry—this was when he'd panicked two months ago, when he'd seen her fully naked for the first time in the nine months they were together and he saw the raised lines along her body and he called her a freak as he scrambled to grab his clothing.

But that Adam wasn't here. The Adam who was with her now was drinking her in and smiling at what he saw.

"Pose for me," he said, his voice husky.

She sprawled on the bed, arranging herself so that she covered her breasts with one arm and crossed her legs to hide what lay between them—nude and yet modest. She smiled at him coyly. "Like this?"

"Oh yeah," he said, grinning. "Just like that."

And then his grin pulled into something cruel, and he called out, "Now!"

The door banged open, and a flood of people rushed inside the bedroom, whooping and shrieking laughter. Cell phones flashed, capturing Missy's shock, immortalizing the scars that were all too clear on her belly, her arms, her thighs. People gathered around her, pointing and chortling, calling her a freak, a slut, a suicide walking. More and more teens pushed inside the small bedroom—Kevin and some of the soccer girls and others, people Missy knew and people Missy didn't know at all, all of them laughing at her, recording her.

And there in the center of it all was Adam, grinning smugly as one of the Matts slipped him a wad of cash.

"Cutterslut!" screamed the other Matt.

"Cutterslut!" came the reply, a dozen voices strong, and growing. "Cutterslut!" The taunt spread until Missy was drowning in a verbal wave. "Cutterslut!" It was a name, a brand, a scarlet letter sliced into her skin.

Half blind from humiliation and fury, Missy scrambled off the bed to grab her clothing. Someone snatched her panties before she could, and another person claimed her boots. Missy barely noticed; the world had given way to a sea of red.

Clutching her clothes to her chest, she tried to push her way out of the room. But she was surrounded by a crush of people, of classmates jeering and clicking pictures. Tears burned her eyes as she frantically tried to shove her way through the mob. But no one would budge.

Missy couldn't breathe.

It was Adam who saved her. "Let her go," he said, his voice like a blade. "She has to go home and cry to her mommy."

The crowd parted, still laughing and mocking.

Missy ran.

She stumbled down the stairs, not stopping to throw on her clothing. She bolted out the door, leaving the taunts of "cutterslut" far behind. As she ran in the Red, an image of Adam burned brightly in her mind—Adam, so smug as he pocketed a wad of cash, grinning hugely, his eyes flashing "gotcha" even as the cell phones captured her forever and longer.

Adam, who had destroyed her over a bet.

Missy ran from her life, thinking now about the salvation that waited for her in her lockbox. She ran, already picturing the razor that would kiss everything away.

She ran, and in her closet at home, the white tie box waited.

CHAPTER 5

Missy stopped long enough to take shelter behind a bush and fumble on her clothing, her scars winking like knives in the moonlight. Stockings and bra, top and skirt, all tugged into place. No boots; those, like her panties, had been reduced to tokens, limited-edition mementos of The Night Adam Ruined Missy's Life. Missy was far too numb to feel the pavement slap against her feet.

Clothed and yet still feeling completely naked, Missy ran back to her house. There was a moment of bitter relief that her key was in her skirt pocket; she would have died of humiliation if her parents or, God forbid, her sister had opened the door. That relief quickly faded as Missy placed the key into the lock.

It fit perfectly, just as Adam had played her perfectly.

He'd played her, and everyone had watched. Those who hadn't seen the live performance were assuredly being treated to the recorded version. Possibly in surround sound.

She thought of everyone—*everyone*—in school seeing her there on that bed, completely bare, her scars and skin on display. She heard their mocking laughter, felt their scorn like pimples erupting on her face.

Oh, God.

The pressure started like a balloon in the middle of her chest, slowly getting bigger. It expanded, flattening her heart, her lungs, now reaching out and around. It cemented her bowels and squeezed her throat as she stood there on the stoop, her hand on the doorknob, tears frozen in her eyes. Her vision blurred. She couldn't get enough air.

The pictures, the video, the gossip—all of it would circulate through school. Everyone either had seen her or would see her, stripped, her sins exposed.

Everyone.

Her hand shaking, she opened the front door and stumbled inside. The scent of garlic and butter had settled in the living room, and Missy breathed in the remnants of dinner as if they could save her.

They couldn't.

Cutterslut.

Adam's eyes, glinting like diamonds. Adam's grin, so horribly smug.

Freak.

Gasping, she worked her way upstairs. She didn't hear the television blaring from her parents' room—which signaled that her mom and dad were having sex—or notice that her sister's bedroom door was wide open, indicating that Sue was out of the house. As far as Missy was concerned, she was alone, for now and for always. She thought she saw a cat from the corner of her eye as she rounded the top of the stairs, but she ignored it because Graygirl was two months dead, and even if it was Graygirl's ghost there in the hallway, the cat couldn't help Missy now.

Only one thing could do that.

Drowning, she staggered into her room and leaned heavily against the door until it shut, then locked it. She turned on the overhead light because her scars, already exposed to everyone, couldn't be shielded by the dark, and she went to her closet door and dragged out her lockbox. She bumped the door semi-closed, and she placed the lockbox carefully on her bed.

Let me make it up to you.

The pressure in her chest had become almost unbearable—the glass jar of her heart had been crushed, the heart inside pulverized—and her breath came only in spastic wheezes. She had a clear thought, clanging like a bell, saying that she didn't need the blade.

But she did. Because without it, she would surely die.

She darted a frantic glance around her room, looking for something she couldn't name. On the closet door, James Dean and Marilyn Monroe said nothing, both lost in the land of stars who had died too young.

She was going to die.

She didn't want to die.

Her hand trembling, she opened her lockbox. Two months dropped away like snowflakes as she stared at the contents within. Before Adam's betrayal—the first betrayal, the one that had merely left her gutted and raw—back when she was cutting frequently, Missy would have gone to the bathroom before she opened her lockbox, and would have rubbed her arms and thighs and stomach with alcohol. But that was another girl, in another lifetime. Potential germs and infection didn't mean anything now.

All that mattered was the blood. She had to bleed out the badness, bleed until she could breathe again.

Folded neatly in the lockbox was a towel, once white, now dingy and stained from her ritual of pain. She took it out, running her fingers over the brown spots, trying to remember them when they had been scarlet drops—fresh, rich, brimming with emotion. It was her own security blanket, a dream catcher that trapped living nightmares when she pressed it against her cuts. The towel protected her from getting caught.

Too late for such things now. She set the towel aside, then looked inside the box.

The razor gleamed, winking like an old friend.

It was the same blade she had always used, taken from a broken disposable razor—the same brand used by her mother. There were times when Missy would touch the razor to her flesh and imagine that her mom knew what she was doing, that they were connected through the steel as if it were an umbilical cord. She would imagine that her mother understood what Missy did and why she did it, that her mother quietly condoned it even as she removed the stubble from her legs.

It was a pleasant lie, and as Missy would float in the quietude that came after the pain, she would enjoy the notion of her mom, even her dad, seeing her true face—that of the real Melissa Miller, whose colors ran outside the lines.

But that was a fantasy. Her parents didn't know her, not really. They went through the motions of affection, smiled the smiles of patience and platitudes. They claimed to accept her for who and what she was, and maybe they even believed they did just that. But her parents had their expectations, and Missy either met those expectations or exceeded them. Anything else was outside of their frame of reference.

The blade was cold to her touch. She stroked it once, hesitant and yet hopeful.

Missy's relationship with her razor wasn't just outside of her parents' frame of reference. It was another language, a dead language of a forgotten tribe. To her parents, pain was something to be avoided at best and dealt with at worst. To Missy, pain was a blessing. It was a moment of crystalline purity, one that made everything somehow bearable, if only for a little while. Momentary agony, and then the buzz of her blood welling up on her flesh. Pain was her salvation; seeing her blood on her skin was like seeing God.

She lifted the razor in her right hand, holding it between her thumb and first two fingers. She heard Adam and the others call her names and accuse her of horrific things, laughing at her all the while. She felt her soul crumple, squeezed into pulp. She tried to breathe and failed.

In her mind, Adam's voice whispered: *Freak*.

Tears stinging her eyes, she sliced down.

▌▌▌▌▌

"Time to go," Death said abruptly. In the blink of an eye, his guitar was nowhere to be found.

Famine smiled tightly, a knife-flash of humor. "From zero to a hundred in a split second."

"It's all in the timing," Death agreed, sounding chipper. "Go thee out unto the world."

The Black Rider would have responded, but Death was already gone.

▌▌▌▌▌

It wasn't enough.

She had sliced her arms to ribbons, but the badness remained, staining her insides like cancer.

She had gouged her belly until it was a mess of meat and blood, but she still couldn't breathe.

She had brought the razor to her inner thighs again and again and again, but with each sting came no release, no comforting numbness that dulled the horror of her life.

It wasn't enough. So she cut again—swiftly, mercilessly.

And maybe it was because her fingers were slick with blood, or maybe it was because she was exhausted and wretched and in excruciating pain, but for whatever the reason, her next stroke—her final stroke—slipped, and she opened up an artery. The spray hit her eyes, her cheek, her chin.

She had a moment of utter shock, in which she let out a quiet "Oh." An inexplicable feeling of déjà vu settled into her bones.

And then the blade slipped from her hand and she sank to the ground and she watched as her life leaked out of her in thick streamers of red.

She wondered numbly what went wrong, and what, if anything, waited for her when it was done. She knew that her parents and sister would think she had committed suicide, and she was horribly sad because she couldn't tell them how wrong they would be. She didn't mean to kill herself. She had only wanted to breathe again.

Bleeding out, Melissa Miller began to die.

You have blood on your hands.

The memories fell upon her, gentle as summer rain: first, Death standing on the doorstep, dressed in delivery browns, telling her to take the package he offered; next, her fingers dragging over the white box, leaving trails of red in their wake; last, Missy grabbing the package and slamming the door in Death's face.

In retrospect, she probably should have been a little more polite.

So afraid. Death's voice again, but she couldn't tell if it was her memory or if Death was with her now. Because he was, wasn't he? She was dying, so he would be there for her, lead her to wherever she was supposed to go . . .

Take the box, Melissa Miller.

The box. Where was the box?

On her closet door, Marilyn Monroe sighed in ecstasy, and James Dean searched for something just out of reach.

The closet. It was in her closet.

She tried to get up and failed; she tried to crawl and instead crashed prone on the floor.

You taking a nap? That was Bella's voice, teasing her on the safety of the soccer field. *You've got to use your body better.*

Listening to Bella, Missy dragged herself across her bedroom floor. Behind her, bloody streaks marred the beige carpet like a serial killer's bread crumbs. Missy made it to her closet door and nudged it open with her wet fingers. She lifted her head up to stare at the top shelf, impossibly high. The long white box that Death had given her was up there, waiting for her to take it and claim what lay inside.

"You should hurry," a cold voice said.

She turned her head—God, when did her head become so heavy? It was too big for her neck—and saw Death seated on her bed, grinning lazily, his eyes sparkling beneath his long messy bangs.

"I'm trying," she whispered.

"You're dying," he corrected. "Try harder."

Missy gritted her teeth and imagined Bella counting her down—*Six seconds, go!*—and propped herself onto her elbows. The world spun. Dizzy, she grabbed on to the door frame and pulled herself up, slowing bringing herself to her knees. She planted one stockinged foot, and using the door frame for balance, she was able to stand. She couldn't feel her feet.

The box was right there, on the edge of the high shelf. She reached up for it and couldn't quite touch it. She thought very, very dark thoughts.

On her bed, Death chuckled. "You're cute when you're going into irreversible shock."

Panting, Missy grabbed a bare hanger. Her fingers were slick with blood, and the hanger nearly slipped free.

Don't drop the ball, she heard Bella scold.

Her arm tingling, her fingers numb, Missy reached up. The hanger brushed against the box, but that wasn't enough to jostle the package loose.

Come on, she thought, *come on!* Maneuvering the hanger, she hooked it under the white box. And then she slowly pulled.

The box slid forward.

Come on! she thought again, her heartbeat pounding in her ears, behind her eyes. She kept pulling the hanger out, excruciatingly slow. The white box crept forward, and now a third of it peeked over the shelf's edge.

Her vision started to dim. Her arm, already heavy, suddenly weighed a thousand pounds and the bones in her legs turned to gelatin. Using the last of her strength, she yanked the hanger out. The momentum pulled the box out farther, and it balanced there on the edge of the shelf for a long moment—tantalizing, untouchable.

And then it crashed to the ground.

Missy didn't feel her legs give out. One moment she was leaning against the door frame, and the next she was sprawled on the floor, the box next to her bloody hand. Her head no longer felt heavy; it was blissfully light, lighter than air, as if it could just float away. The pain from her cuts had vanished, like magic, and so had the feeling in her limbs. Sweat dotted her brow, gleaming among the spatter of blood by her eyes.

She was so very cold. So very tired.

"Either take the box, Melissa Miller, or take thy rest." Death's words echoed in her bones, frosted her soul. His voice soft, he commanded: "Choose now."

Choose.

Missy rolled her head to stare at the package on the floor next to her. The box was longer than she had remembered, and she briefly wondered how it had fit atop her closet. *Doesn't matter how,* she decided as she dragged her hand over to the fallen box. *It fit because it was supposed to fit.*

Just like she was supposed to take the box.

As her fingers brushed against it, the white package turned the red of ripe cherries.

She couldn't see Death, but she heard the smile in his cold, cold voice. "The choice is made. Open the box, Melissa Miller."

With those words, heat flooded her limbs, bringing with it newfound strength. Missy, no longer dying, rolled onto her hip and pushed herself up until she was on her knees. The cheerfully red package lay in front of her like a birthday present. She lifted the lid off the box.

Inside, a sword rested against a backing of ruby-colored cloth. The weapon looked nothing like its more modern cousins; for one thing, it was too short, and for another, it wasn't steel or iron but something redder, like bronze. The straight blade plumped in the middle, with one end coming to a wicked point and the other extending into a hilt. It was the *idea* of a sword, there in its once white box.

"Oh," Missy breathed, enamored. The sword radiated age and, stronger than that, power, and as she stared at it raptly, she felt something akin to awe wash over her. This blade was no mere sword—it was a Sword, meant to be revered.

"It's beautiful," she whispered.

"It's yours."

"Mine?" Impossible. She couldn't own such a treasure.

"Yours," said Death. "The Sword is your symbol of office."

That got Missy to tear her gaze from the weapon in its box and stare at the figure on her bed. He bore more than a passing resemblance to a certain dead alternative rock star, but Missy understood that his appearance was nothing more than a whim. He sat there in a red and black striped sweater, frayed along the hem of one of the sleeves, the collar of a white shirt jutting out along the neckline. His blue jeans were torn and patched; his Converse sneakers looked comfortably broken in. Everything about him, from his outfit to the messy long blond hair, appeared casual, familiar.

Everything except his eyes. Beneath the startling blue, they were bottomless. She could get lost in those eyes and never know it until she was already far, far gone. His eyes were haunting.

"Thou art War," Death said, his voice cold and, appropriately, grave. "Thou art the Red Rider of the Apocalypse." And then, warmer: "Rock on."

Missy opened her mouth and then closed it with an audible snap.

War.

She knew she shouldn't be calmly sitting on her bedroom floor, being told by Death—by a very attractive Death—that she was now War of the Apocalypse. She knew she should be terrified. She realized she might be certifiably insane. She understood all of this, and none of it mattered.

She beheld the weapon in its box, and she longed to touch it, to feel its weight in her hands. No, it wasn't just a weapon. It was power incarnate; it was passion given form. It was glorious.

And it was *hers*.

"Yes," Death said. "It is."

It didn't even make her blink that Death had read her mind; this was a day in which the impossible was accepted as commonplace. She stared at the blade in its cherry-red box, and she felt it staring back, assessing her. Accepting her. She was War, and the weapon, *her* weapon, called to her, its voice a metallic song that reverberated in her mind like the clang of steel against steel. It was hypnotic.

"Pick up the Sword. Feel its weight in your hand," Death said. And then, as an afterthought: "And brace yourself."

Missy closed her fingers around the handle and lifted the Sword free from its box.

Emotions slammed into her, riding her body and screaming

along her skin. Anger in its various forms took her first, chewed her up and spat her out: fury, scalding and insistent; jealousy, a gnawing hunger; hatred, cold enough to freeze her blood. Happiness, then, had its turn, soothing her where rage had left scorch marks: joy, blissful and light; kindness, a warm balm; the giddy touch of glee; a tickle of contentment. Love washed over her in a gentle rain, only to burn her as it transformed into lust and, hotter still, ecstasy. On its heels came the soft chill of vulnerability, and the wrenching emptiness of shame.

All of that and more, all in the space of one breath to the next.

Missy's body jittered as the elations and sorrows of every living thing jolted through her like lightning. She tried to scream but couldn't do more than grit her teeth against the tidal wave of sensation.

Control, Death whispered in her mind.

Control? That was a bitter joke. Proof of that was tattooed along her arms and legs and stomach.

You cut yourself in reaction to an abundance of emotion, Death said, unflappable. *Act instead of react. Control.*

Tears squeezed from her eyes as she pushed against the Sword, against the surge of emotion. It was like trying to hold back an avalanche with her fingers. She couldn't do this.

"Of course you can," Death said aloud. "You have before."

She thought of the glass jar of her heart, how it would bottle her rage and sorrow and aching embarrassment and allow her to swim through her life without being pulled under.

Of *course* she could do this. She had been doing it for months.

Snarling, she pushed once again, shoving the emotions back

into the Sword. They flowed off her like wasps washed away in a sudden storm, stinging her even as they rushed past. By the time she was done, she was sweating freely and shaking like a junkie.

And damn if she didn't feel *good*.

The Sword, perhaps in reaction to her catharsis, winked . . . and transformed into a long silver sword with a flared cross guard. The hilt now sported a leather-wrapped handle, oxblood red, counterbalanced by a circular silver pommel.

Grinning, Missy hefted the blade high. It was neither too heavy nor too light, and it felt as if it had been forged specifically for her hand.

The Sword hummed in her grip, singing of blood and fury, of passion unrestrained. As she brandished it, the weapon showed her visions of the world tearing itself apart in its need to uncover a savior, images of a figure in red—of Missy—holding the Sword aloft like a beacon on a stormy night.

Yes, she thought joyously. *Yes*. That was the truth of it: everyone, *everything*, was filled with wants and needs and urges, and most people spent their lives denying themselves, talking themselves into stifling banality. They didn't realize how they were suffocating their potential until it was nothing more than a stillborn dream. With the Sword, Missy could show them the truth, and more. She could spread the gospel of war and lead them to enlightenment. They would meet their savior in a river of blood.

She let out a ferocious laugh, one that left her throat raw.

"Control," murmured Death.

Oh, she was in control. More control now than ever before.

His voice, like a caress: "Are you, now?"

Yes.

Her gaze was transfixed on the Sword, and she drew it close to her face. She saw herself reflected in the blade: her eyes shone wickedly, hinting of murder, and her smile was twisted into something grotesque. She blinked and the reflection vanished, replaced by the glimmer of cold steel.

The dark vision acted like a splash of ice water, quickly sobering her. She dropped the Sword as if burned, and it landed on the blood-streaked carpet with a muffled thump. The Sword's image lingered behind her eyes, and she shuddered violently. She whispered, "What was that?"

"You. Nothing more, nothing less."

She turned to face Death, who was sitting up on her bed, watching her intently. Part of her squirmed from that considering gaze . . . but another part of her, the one that had relished holding the Sword, enjoyed his attention. More than enjoyed it, based on her body's reaction. She crossed her arms over her chest. Her voice husky, she said, "That wasn't me."

"You are War. The passions of all living things call to you, and you to them. And your own passions are more . . . extreme." He emphasized the last word, turning it into something enticing.

She rubbed her arms, even though she wasn't cold. If anything, she was feeling much, much too warm. "You picked the wrong person. I'm just a—"

Freak, Adam jeered.

"—a girl," she said bitterly.

Death smiled, a slow curving of his lips that made Missy's heart beat faster. "Your past is meaningless," he said, "and your future is waiting to be defined. Don't condemn yourself to mediocrity just yet."

His words rang with the promise of salvation, and for a wonderful moment, Missy felt hope bloom.

But then she thought suddenly of Graygirl, heard the cat's final, pitiful cry before she died in Missy's arms.

Missy's eyes burned with unshed tears. She wanted to curse, to shout, to beg for forgiveness, but the words refused to come. No matter what Death said, her past couldn't be erased. She bore her sins like scars.

"That's one thing I'll never understand," said Death, shaking his head. "Why do you people insist on suffering?"

Missy had no answer.

"Don't feel bad. I don't have an answer, either, and I've been doing this for a long, long time." He held out his hand to her.

Missy took a deep breath, and then she accepted Death's hand. It was firm, and cool, and as he helped her to her feet, a gentle numbness spread through her body, as if her dead face had encased her like a mummy.

"Come on," Death said, smiling softly. "The night is young, and there's much to do."

Missy followed Death out of her room, feeling as if she were traveling in a dream. Around her, the world was out of sync—she heard her parents in their bedroom, the sounds of their love-making tinny and peppered with static; the photographs on the walls had faded into background floaters, their colors leeched away. Missy's head buzzed, not unpleasantly, as she noticed these oddities. It made sense that the mundane trappings of the world appeared dim and out of reach; by accepting the Sword, Missy had become more real, perhaps even surreal. It wasn't that she was alone because no one could relate to her; rather, she had transcended the glamour of the ordinary.

It was possible, she reflected, that the soda she'd had at Kevin's party had been laced with something exotic and she was tripping her fool head off.

Death glided sinuously down the stairs, and Missy drifted after him, a fleshy balloon filled with helium kisses. She was filthy and shoeless, and that was irrelevant. She had nearly died, and that, too, was irrelevant. She was War, the Red Rider of the Apocalypse. She was beyond concerns of bare feet and grime. Melissa Miller followed where Death walked, leaving her life behind her.

They came to a halt by her front door. Death glanced back at her, an unreadable smile on his face. "War," he said, "meet thy steed." And then he opened the door and motioned outside.

At the bottom of the front stoop, a horse waited.

Missy sucked in a startled breath. She had seen horses before, but none of them had come close to the powerful creature standing in her front yard. Tall to the point of monstrosity, proud to the point of nobility, it stood, limbs locked, nostrils flared. From muzzle to mane to flank, it was the color of spilled blood—all but the eyes, which were the black of nightmares. Missy felt the horse's hatred slap her, sensed its silent dare for her to approach.

No, not a dare. It was *hoping* she would step forward. It wanted to tear her apart.

How on earth was she supposed to ride *that?*

"Warhorse," said Death cheerfully, "meet thy Rider."

The steed bared its teeth. Its very sharp-looking teeth.

Missy paled, and she took an involuntary step backward.

"I wouldn't do that," Death murmured. "If it thinks you're afraid, it will attack. Then things will get messy."

She froze. Her heart tried to leap out of her mouth and instead got lodged in her throat.

"It's a bit temperamental," Death said, perhaps by way of apology. "But it's a fine steed."

The warhorse snorted.

Missy swallowed thickly. The horse had understood Death; she would have bet her life on it. Which, she supposed, she already had. Her voice reedy, she said, "Don't suppose I could have a motorcycle instead."

That made Death chuckle. "Don't suppose you have a license for a motorcycle."

Okay, he had a point.

Death motioned to the red horse. "Gentle thy steed, War."

She quashed an insane urge to laugh. He made it sound so easy. Clean your room. Do your homework. Gentle your warhorse. "I have no idea how to do that."

"You'll figure it out."

Missy stared at the horse as it radiated fury. "And if I don't?"

"Then your tenure as War will be cut quite short," Death said, sounding horribly chipper. "And you go right back to dying."

"Oh." No pressure or anything. "Okay then."

A minute passed as Missy tried to think of how to approach the horse without losing a hand, and she came up blank. Wasn't there something that went in their mouths to keep them from biting? And reins to steer? And a saddle? What was she supposed to do, magically fly up onto the horse and pray for the best?

As she stared at the horse in its silent rage, the calming numbness that had filled her since she had taken Death's hand began to ebb. She couldn't even control her own emotions; how was she supposed to control an ill-tempered horse? Her breath threatened to hitch, so she held it tight tight tight until she finally had to release it in a long, shaky exhalation.

"War," Death said, all traces of humor gone. "Gentle thy steed."

The horse snorted again. At her.

Let her go. She has to go home and cry to her mommy.

White hot fury flared through her, charring her heart and searing the marrow in her bones. She might not know the first thing about horses, but she recognized scorn when she heard it. Before her life had taken a turn for the supernatural, she would have either ignored the derision and the pain that came with it, or she would have attacked in kind with verbal slashes. After everything that had happened tonight, she wasn't about to back down from a freaking *horse*, no matter how terrifying it was. Staring hard at the red steed, she cemented her dead face over her features.

SHOW IT YOUR STRENGTH.

That wasn't Death's voice—his was cold and yet intimate, like a snowflake melting on her tongue. This voice was a heated whisper threaded with licks of fire. It was the voice of the Sword, which was back in her room where she had dropped it . . . and yet it was still with her, murmuring to her. Standing outside in the midnight air, in her stockinged feet and rumpled clothing, she felt the Sword's presence in her mind as it waited for her to summon it. This wasn't the suffocating, spiraling pressure of being completely overwhelmed; the closest thing she could compare it to was the comfortable, familiar weight of a favorite cat on her lap.

In a blink, she thought of Graygirl—not of the sickly creature she had become, but the majestic cat she had been in her prime. She remembered how Graygirl had felt in her lap as she did her homework, and how the cat had curled next to her in bed, a purring puff ball nuzzled in the crook of Missy's arm.

In her mind, the Sword purred as she imagined herself stroking the weapon gently, almost lovingly.

STRENGTH, the Sword repeated.

Missy gazed at the steed coldly. People rode horses, she told herself. They muzzled horses and saddled them and controlled them with reins and spurs. *I will ride you,* she silently promised the horse. She stepped forward.

The red steed pawed the ground once, twice.

Missy kept her gaze on the animal as she quietly moved to the right. She stayed out of range of its mouth and legs as she slowly circled it, appreciating how large the horse was, how it emanated power. The red tail swished once as she passed by, and she gave the raised rear leg a respectable berth. As she completed the circuit, the horse snapped its teeth at her.

Dead face unflinching, Missy stomped her foot, hard.

The horse's ears flattened back.

Missy shook her head, the motion exaggerated, as if she were slicing the air with her chin. She wasn't having any of that, not from her horse. *You hear me, horse? You're mine. Behave.*

The red steed's ears quivered, then flicked toward her.

Missy began moving again, circling the steed. This time, it didn't threaten to kick her as she passed its hindquarters. Better. She walked by its right shoulder, noting how its neck was arched high, its muscles tight. The horse was tense, anticipating. In a burst of intuition, she realized it was waiting for something.

In her mind, the Sword sang of blood and violence.

Ah.

Her dead face secure, Missy bottled her heart and held out her hand. She told the Sword, *Come to me.*

The weapon appeared in a blink, hovering just over her palm. *Yes,* she thought, appreciating the way the blade caught the gleam of moonlight. *Yes.* Missy wrapped her fingers around the hilt, and adrenaline surged through her, bringing her blood to a boil. She wanted to dance, to move, to slam her foot against a soccer ball—to rip a tree up from its roots and throw it into the heavens.

And she *could.* With the Sword in her hand, she could do anything.

Anything at all.

Control, whispered a still, small voice, as soft as death.

Yes, control. Missy was in control. She pointed her symbol of office at the steed. The wicked point ended just beneath the animal's chin. It stood very, very still.

"Hello, little horse," she said, her voice like thunder. "I'm War."

The horse blew air out its nostrils in a quick burst, its breath fogging the steel blade. Its ears twitched.

"And you're my steed."

The horse let out a soft nicker. Then it snorted once as it stepped backward, just out of range of the Sword's point, and it bowed its head.

Missy wanted to whoop for joy. Instead she allowed herself a very small smile.

"Told you you'd figure it out," said Death.

She lowered the Sword and approached the horse, which kept its head low. Visions whirled in her mind, showing her the red steed with its Rider as they traveled on land faster than a train, flying through the air like a comet, slicing across the turbulent seas—War and her steed, together, leaving their imprint on the world like hoofmarks in mud.

Lost in memories that weren't hers, Missy sheathed her Sword. She didn't see it vanish as she slid it to rest, and because its presence glowed contently in her mind, she didn't feel its physical departure. Her gaze was transfixed on the horse, her horse, and as she ran her hand over its powerful neck, she marveled at the strength she felt beneath her fingers.

"You put other horses to shame," she said softly. "You're magnificent."

The steed blew air through its nose, acknowledging the compliment.

"You're feeding its ego," Death said.

Missy smiled proudly. "It should have an ego. It's amazing." She paused, her fingers rubbing its shoulder. "What's its name?"

"It is the red steed. It needs no name, War."

Missy imagined a life of being called "horse." Well, no wonder it had an attitude. "I think you should have a name," she said to her steed. "I'll call you Ares."

The horse craned its neck so that it was looking at Missy, and it let out a satisfied snort.

"You named it after a god?" Death laughed. "I did mention its ego, didn't I?"

Ares leveled a stare at Death, who laughed even louder.

"Don't mind him," Missy said to the horse, stroking its back. "He's just jealous." How could she have ever thought her steed's eyes were frightening? They were dual onyxes, shining with liquid emotion.

She heard movement behind her even as Ares neighed in warning. Missy turned abruptly, summoning the Sword as she did so, rational thought giving way to the instinct for violence. But Death was right there in front of her, kissing-close, making her weapon useless. His face was blank, masklike, all but his eyes. Emotions swirled in their depths, too quick and deep for Missy to name.

Her mouth went painfully dry. How could she have forgotten who—no, *what*—he was? She'd turned her back on Death, had all but insulted him, all because she was enamored of her warhorse—the horse *he* had given her, along with her Sword. Death had come calling, bearing gifts, and she had repaid him with casual contempt.

She remembered, suddenly, how she had slammed the door in his face.

Oh God.

Missy swallowed thickly. Her head was too light; her bladder, too full. Her world tunneled down to a series of don'ts: *Don't scream, don't pee, don't pass out.*

Death leaned in and Missy arched back, coming to rest against Ares' side. She tried to speak, but her words caught in her throat, strangling her. Now Death was nose to nose with her, and she breathed in the smells of fresh earth and old paper, and beneath that, something primal that had no name. It was a heady mixture, that combination of power and comfort and age, and Missy found herself breathing too fast . . . and not entirely due to fear.

Is this a death wish? she wondered, and then she fought back a nervous giggle.

A touch like frost as Death stroked her cheek, once, his cold fingers tracing the curve of her face.

"This is why I've always liked you," he murmured, dropping his hand. "You're saucy."

His words tripped along her spine, making her shiver. "Me?"

"You. War." Something in his gaze softened. "The others who have ridden before you."

"There've been others?" she blurted. "Like me?"

"Oh, yes," he said, a knowing smile teasing his lips. "War and Death have always worked well together."

Worked?

Oh.

A flush of warmth crept over her face where Death's fingers had been . . . and that warmth reached lower, making her knees buckle. If not for Ares, she would have crashed to the ground.

Unless, of course, Death would have caught her.

Still gazing at Missy, he reached over to pat the warhorse. Missy felt Ares shudder beneath his touch. "Treat thy steed well," said Death, "and it will repay you in kind."

That sounded more like a command than advice. Her reply came out in a choked whisper: "I will."

"Well, then. Saddle up, Red Rider," Death said, stepping back to give her space. "Time to earn your keep."

She struggled to get her heartbeat down from its rocketing speed to something less likely to put her in cardiac arrest. She breathed, and breathed again, and slowly her body calmed. Her mind, though, was a mess of thoughts and feelings—confusion, primarily, with snatches of embarrassment and, inexplicably, jealousy. Of course there had been others who had been War. The notion shouldn't bother her. "What am I supposed to do?"

"Thou art War," Death replied. "Go thee out unto the world."

Missy waited, but no explanation followed. She took a deep breath as she sheathed her Sword, this time noticing how the blade simply vanished. Missy blinked, then blinked again, and finally turned to face Ares. "Want to go for a ride?"

The horse knelt low enough for Missy to pull herself onto its back. As she settled down, she realized that there was a saddle beneath her and reins in her hands. She had no idea if she had magicked up the gear or if Ares had—or, for that matter, if Death had—so she just took it in stride. One thing she was quickly learning this night was to roll with the supernatural punches.

And touches.

Shivering in her seat, she saw that Death, too, was astride a horse—one that had, apparently, stepped out of nowhere. Or maybe it had been invisible until now. Or maybe she simply hadn't noticed it before this moment. Or maybe none of those things. Atop his pale steed, Death grinned.

Roll with it, Missy.

She rolled with it. "Okay," she said aloud. "Let's go."

Ares reared back, and Missy clutched the reins for dear life. She hung suspended, her thoughts tumbling together—

—I'm in the air oh God don't let me fall don't oh God I can't breathe my chest hurts my heart oh God my heart is pounding through my ribs and I'm still holding on still holding and I'm not falling and look and me look look my God look this is so damn COOL—

—and as the nighttime air kissed her face she let out a jubilant shout, which the warhorse matched with a trumpeting whinny.

And then both Rider and steed took off into the night.

CHAPTER 7

Melissa Miller, the most powerful sixteen-year-old in the universe, rode through the skies atop her fiery red steed. Bruised from the wind, Missy grinned wide enough to split her face. This was roller coaster giddiness and freefall elation—better than ferociously defending the goal in soccer, or acing a test, or even that magical first kiss. This was the epitome of exhilaration, all white bubbles tickling her skin. This, in other words, was the most incredible thing that had ever happened to her. They soared, and beneath them, the world waited.

Missy wanted to see more. The warhorse, either intuiting or understanding its Rider's intent, swooped lower, giving Missy a bird's-eye view of a slumbering city. Pinpricks of light pierced the nighttime darkness, illuminating occasional houses and the rare open business. Parked cars littered the roads like children's toys, scattered and forgotten. Wherever they were, it was too late to be night and too early to be morning. Missy blinked, and they left the city far behind. Ares climbed higher, and soon the world was once again a smudge beneath them.

Missy's laughter was eaten by the wind.

They thundered across the sky, shredding clouds, galloping faster than time itself. All too soon, Ares banked and dropped low, spiraling quickly, with Missy clinging to the reins and shrieking in terrified delight. Another cityscape bloomed beneath them, this one beating back the nighttime darkness with numerous streetlamps. Cars moved like sluggish beetles. People in the street were nothing more than fleas, nearly invisible but still present.

Now along with the sheer joy of flying, Missy felt the stirrings of something else, something more viscous. It rose up, congealing the white bubbles of exhilaration into thick blotches of red anticipation. She bottled her heart and reaffixed her dead face. Thus girded for battle, Missy opened herself up to the power of War.

This time, the emotions didn't hit her; they nibbled at her, taking tiny bites and attempting to burrow under her flesh like ticks. Here, a bit of joy; there, a mouthful of sorrow. She felt them all, felt their pain and pity and excitement and boredom, and she relished the sensations along her skin, even as she plucked them off and singed them in ghostly fingers.

It was the small wars, though, that rippled pleasant shocks through her: kisses of domestic violence, shivers of gang activity, thrills of verbal abuse. That last in particular left her trembling in ecstasy: the barbed tongues and heated lashes, the snide comments with their blistering aftermath, all of it thrummed along her skin, leaving it tingling. She let out an "Ummm" as, in one house far below, someone drank and drank to dull the agony of overwhelming heartbreak.

Adam's voice, all silky perfection: *Let me make it up to you.*

She growled, the sound filled with the promise of bloodshed. Oh, he'd make it up to her, all right. She wanted her pound of flesh.

"Take me to the party," she told Ares, and then she gave her horse the address. The steed whinnied in response and took off like a gunshot. In her building rage, Missy didn't realize she was trailing emotional flotsam. Even if she did, she wouldn't have cared. Missy was in the Red, in the place where pain was pleasure and mouths were lined with razors. She streaked away, leaving behind feelings of cruel determination that fell upon the city below like acid rain.

Her casual disregard would prompt six cases of vandalism, eight muggings, two car crashes, and thirty-one trips to the emergency room.

Melissa Miller would have torn out her heart if she knew she was the cause of such violence. War, however, would have shrugged it off either as collateral damage or as part of the job. The Red Rider wasn't concerned with the human toll of war; that, ultimately, was Death's province.

Smiling coldly, her eyes bright with visions of destruction, Missy held tight to Ares and waited to be delivered to her former love.

████

The party was still in full swing, for which Missy was profoundly grateful. She had many things to say to Adam and his cohorts, and she meant to let her body do the talking.

The warhorse landed in Kevin's front lawn, amid a group of scattershot teens clumped like weeds. None of them reacted to either the steed or Missy; they all continued talking and laughing as they unobtrusively moved back, sloshing the liquid in their cups as they gave the horse a wide berth.

Cool, Missy thought. She'd gone through the last two months at high school wanting to be invisible. Now, apparently, she had gotten her wish. An ugly smile warped her mouth into a parody of humor. Oh, the things she could do to Adam if he couldn't see her . . .

The horse snorted.

"You're right," she murmured, patting its neck. "Why imagine it when I can do it?" Not that she actually understood the steed, but what else could it have meant? She was War, after all. Time to make with the warring.

She slid off of Ares, taking a moment to get her balance. Riding in the sky had been a thrill, but it was good to be back on the ground. The grass of the front lawn was damp beneath her stockinged feet, but not unpleasantly so.

Next time, she told herself, *wear shoes. And panties.*

Knees bent, she bounced loosely until her legs were comfortable with her weight again. Then she stood tall, taking in the gossip of teens, the music thumping from behind the closed front door, the house itself. So very normal. So very ordinary. Gone was the anxiety she had felt when she'd approached earlier tonight. She let her dead face crash to the ground, and she stomped it into a thousand shards.

Let the leeches look upon her. She would salt them in righteous fury.

Missy smiled coldly as she summoned her Sword. It settled into her hand quietly, comfortably, ready to entice people to slaughter.

The people nearest Missy—two guys and three girls, all seniors—immediately recoiled as if slapped. One of the girls became noisily, violently sick right there in the front yard, and one of the guys peed himself, which was disguised by his drink slipping from his shaking hand and splashing his shirt and pants. The other teens outside, to a person suddenly uneasy, jeered at their classmates, loud in their derision and silently thankful they weren't the recipients of such attention.

Missy watched the spectacle for a few seconds, first amused, then quickly bored. She wasn't here for them. Already thinking of how she would greet Adam, she turned to Ares and commanded, "Behave."

The steed blinked its obsidian eyes.

"Don't kill anyone," Missy clarified. "Or eat anyone." After a moment's consideration, she added, "Or hurt anyone."

Ares blew through its nostrils once, loudly.

She patted its shoulder. "I promise to let you trample his carcass when I'm done. All right?"

The horse let out an equine sigh.

Missy decided that meant agreement. She hefted the Sword over her shoulder and padded her way to the front door. Around her, tempers shortened. Partygoers, already feeling tense, started to get angry—the booze was running low; the music sucked; nothing about tonight was going as planned. More than one person abruptly decided they had been there and done that, so they pitched their cups onto the grass and stormed away, complaining loudly about how lame the party was. Missy nudged past one guy—a football hero, based on his letter jacket—and he shoved another guy out of his space. That second guy accidentally jostled the girl next to him, spilling his drink down her shirt. She shrieked and slapped him, which got him to yelling about her lack of intelligence, her need for hygiene, and her questionable parentage.

And that was all without Missy doing anything other than summoning her Sword.

Smiling sweetly as she imagined using her weapon to slice Adam into ribbons, she pushed open the door and entered the house.

It was still littered with people, many of whom she recognized as her fellow juniors. The music pounded an angry beat, and Missy approved, nodding her head in time to the drums as she meandered around the living room, searching for Adam. She dragged the Sword behind her, and it left sparks of fury in her wake.

Missy walked unnoticed, but her presence was felt by every person in the room:

Erica, still sickened by the way Missy had been used but unable to bring herself to leave the party, wrapped her arms around herself and started scraping her thumbnails over her forearms, drawing blood . . .

Jenna, she of the fabulous shredded red skirt that Missy had admired, glowered at one of the other varsity soccer girls in the clique who'd had the nerve to flirt with Matt Higgins, knowing full well that Jenna'd had her eye on Matt for ages, so Jenna made a catty remark about the girl's poor attempt to cover her bumper crop of pimples, and the others in the clique screeched laughter even as the girl blushed in shame and rage . . .

Matt, who had coined the term "cutterslut," glared sullenly at the star quarterback, knowing he was the one who'd scratched Matt's custom paint job on his car but unable to prove it, and damn if the guy wasn't smirking at him, the bastard . . .

Missy thought about cutting Matt down right there in front of everyone, about taking the Sword and oiling its blade with his blood. But no—she was saving that murderous impulse for Adam. So instead, she smiled wickedly and blew Matt a kiss.

That's when Matt decided he'd had enough of the quarter-back's sneer and crumpled his empty beer can and pitched it at the guy's head. The football star got in Matt's face. Words clashed. And then the quarterback popped Matt in the eye.

Around them, kids cheered as the fight got under way. Someone started the chant "Fight! Fight! Fight!" and now everyone was doing it, even Erica with her scratched arms and Jenna with her sharp tongue. Kevin, the party god himself, got between Matt and the other guy, telling them to take it outside for God's sake, because if the house got totaled his dad would kill him, and then he caught a fist in the teeth for his trouble. The spectators, frenzied, cheered louder. Blood was in the air.

Missy sidestepped the brawling teens and continued her search for Adam.

In the kitchen, groups of people clustered around the mostly empty punch bowl. Missy frowned, remembering how Adam had come up behind her as she'd taken a can of Cherry Coke. Around her, the teens shivered . . . and then one of them, suddenly convinced another girl had started a vicious rumor about her, grabbed the target of her rage by her hair and shoved her face into the punch bowl. Shouts and laughter erupted around them, and it wasn't until Missy walked out that someone realized the girl with her face in the punch bowl was drowning.

||||||

Outside, the red steed stood at attention, waiting for its mistress to return. It ignored the humans around it as a giant would ignore a smattering of gnats, and it entertained itself with memories of battles past. It pretended that beneath its hooves the ground was slippery with spilled guts, that its ears rang pleasantly with the music of murder. It hoped its mistress was serious about giving it a carcass to trample, but War was known for a sharp sense of humor that the steed didn't quite understand. Humor was a subtle thing, dependent on nuances and emotional inflections. Such things were beyond the horse. It saw the world in terms of black and white.

And red, of course. And red.

It gazed at one human who got too close to it, and it was sorely tempted to bite off the creature's hand. But its mistress told it not to hurt anyone. The steed was certain that even if it cauterized the wound as its teeth sliced through flesh and bone, the action would cause great pain—indeed, pain would have been the point. So it merely watched the human, and it imagined the taste of blood and marrow in its mouth.

Beneath its hooves, weeds slowly choked the grass.

||||||

Missy paraded through the house, musing over the different scents of anger. There was the peppery smell of irritation, and the mustard spice of slow fury. Bitterness smacked of garlic, and resentment was the cloying odor of burned chocolate. She walked, taking in the aromas of reaction, and around her, people fumed.

Adam was nowhere to be found on the first floor.

Missy marched up the stairs, and the sounds of fighting faded to background noise. The handful of teens loitering in the upstairs hallway started arguing as Missy approached; as she walked by them, they replaced words with fists. By the time one of them took a tumble down the stairs, Missy had entered one of the bedrooms.

The same bedroom where Adam had fooled her so completely.

Another boy was on the bed, doing things with a girl that should have made Missy blush. Their limbs were pretzeled together, their bodies undulating, skin on skin, keeping time to the creaking of the bedsprings. Missy watched, and she blinked away the unbidden memory of her and Adam back when things were good, the two of them wrapped tightly and exploring each other with fingers and mouths. She sucked in a heated breath as she remembered the feeling of him on her, of him in her, and for a long moment her world went red.

Looking hot under all the black.

Missy shuddered, shedding the memory and the feeling like snakeskin.

On the bed, the boy became more aggressive. His fluid, almost tender movements now were jerky thrusts. The girl enjoyed it, based on the animal sounds erupting from her mouth. She speared him with her nails, lacerating his shoulders, his back, his bottom. He was too caught up in his own passion to notice the stings of his lover's affection.

Missy figured he'd notice in the morning when he tried to sit down. She left them to their grunting.

In the next bedroom, the scene was much the same . . . except it was two girls.

As for the master bedroom, well, Missy was sure Kevin's parents would sooner burn the bed than sleep on it if they had seen what Missy witnessed. She never would have guessed that Trudy, the fullback on the varsity soccer team, was that limber.

Amusing, yes. Educational, even. But without Adam there, it was pointless. She growled in frustration, and around her the partygoers snarled in anger. Her former boyfriend wasn't at the party. For all she knew, she had just missed him.

She slammed her fist against the wall. Next to her, two students launched themselves at each other, spittle and fists flying. By the time they were separated, one of them had a fractured hand, and the other sported a split lip and broken teeth. Neither of them could explain why they had started fighting; all they could say is they just *had to* feel their knuckles pounding another person's body into raw meat. Missy didn't see any of it; she was already down the stairs when the first punch landed.

She thought of Adam—of his eyes glinting like diamonds; his smile, filled with barbed-wire teeth.

I'm coming for you, she promised him silently. *I'm coming.*

Outside once again, she meandered around the clumps of shrieking teens as they fought and taunted one another. Their sounds washed over her, splashed her in crimson drops of rage. Her schoolmates screamed like rabbits, and Missy basked in their howls. It occurred to her, as she approached her waiting steed, that when everyone screamed, you couldn't tell who was the football hero and who was the nerd, who was the head cheerleader and who was the band geek. Violence smashed through societal expectations and exposed people at their core—and at their core, they were all the same. Fury, Missy decided, made people honest.

In her hand, the Sword gleamed as if in agreement.

Missy stroked Ares' neck, thinking wistfully of murder. When she found Adam, she would show him just how much she had been thinking about him. She'd carve her name onto his stomach, brand her kiss on his back. She'd paint his world red in vicious, meaty streaks.

He's probably home, she thought, nodding to herself. So that would be where she went next: his house. And if he wasn't there, well, someone would know how to find him. Missy would just have to ask nicely. She'd use the Sword to punctuate the question.

She heard sirens in the distance. Maybe the police were finally en route to break up the party, possibly joined by an ambulance or two, coming to tote revelers away to the land of IV drips and white cotton sheets. Nothing like a little jaunt to the police station or the hospital to really build character.

Missy smiled tightly as she sheathed her Sword. Ares pawed the ground, and Missy mistook her steed's action for impatience. "Don't worry," she told the horse. "We'll find him, even if it takes all night."

From behind her: "This is how you squander your power?"

The speaker's voice squeezed Missy's stomach, leaving her suddenly, overwhelmingly ravenous.

She turned to face a woman seated atop a midnight-black horse. The woman—cadaverously thin, and covered head to toe in black, from her wide-brimmed hat to her trench coat to her boots—held an old-fashioned set of scales in one gloved hand.

Missy stared at those scales, and though she didn't recognize them, War snarled a silent challenge.

"I shouldn't be surprised," the woman said. "You've always been one to flaunt yourself like a whore."

Wide-eyed, Missy asked, "Who *are* you?"

"The Black Rider, wielder of the Scales and blight of abundance." The woman in black flashed a smile, her teeth small and white and perfect. "But you may call me Famine."

CHAPTER 8

The cacophony around them was nothing more than static, the chaos of violence reduced to an afterthought. There was the woman in black on her horse, and there was Ares, and there was Missy herself—that was the entirety of the world.

The woman called Famine looked Missy up and down, that dark gaze measuring Missy's worth down to the pound. Missy's stomach plummeted to her toes. It wasn't just that the black-clad woman could see her when others could not, although the naked hunger in the woman's pitiless eyes left Missy's heart pounding. It was the sheer power radiating from the whipcord-thin form that reduced Missy's confidence to ash. This was no brute show of strength, bludgeoning Missy into submission; this was a subtle display, the insidious tug of undertow. It pulled her under, squeezing her like a sponge, wringing out her life.

God, she was so hungry.

Stop, Missy tried to say, but her words fell stillborn from her lips.

Famine watched her silently, her face smooth, her mouth pressed into a thin line.

Missy, dizzy with the need to eat, stumbled backward. If not for Ares standing just behind her, she would have fallen to her knees. She reached for her steed and drew in a shuddering breath. Her fingers threaded the warhorse's rough coat, and she whispered, "Help me."

Ares lunged, snapping its teeth at the black horse. Famine's steed reared back, out of range of those powerful jaws. The woman in black—still holding her scales in one hand—managed to keep her balance. When her horse came down, she spoke softly to it, quieting it. In those moments of distraction, Missy's hunger abated.

Missy murmured to Ares as she stroked it, thanking the horse for its help. She barely heard the steed's snort of acknowledgment; her thoughts were dust motes in a windstorm, scattered and powerless. Part of her wanted to flee, to climb atop Ares and take to the sky, leaving the shadowed woman far behind. But another part wanted to see how the woman's smile looked after Missy punched out her teeth. She clenched her fist, imagining the feeling of flesh against flesh—the give of muscle, the crunch of bone. She could almost smell the tang of blood, the woman's blood, spicing the air.

Her chest was too tight.

She wanted to hurt the woman, to erase her features with her fists and see what lay beneath her skin. And more than hurt—she wanted to draw her Sword and carve a second mouth along the woman's throat, a new mouth that was wet and red and gaping. She wanted Famine's death rattle to sing her to sleep.

Missy's chest constricted, and she couldn't take a proper breath. *No,* she wheezed. *No. That's not me.* She needed her blade, right now. She had to cut and cut and cut until she could think again, breathe again.

But she *did* have a blade, didn't she? It wasn't in her hand, but she still felt it in her mind, reverberating, clamoring to be heard. She listened as the Sword sang to her with the clarity of steel, the simplicity of bloodshed.

Slowly, her panic ebbed. Though her chest was still too tight and her heart was beating too fast, she no longer felt the overwhelming need to open her veins in the moonlight and bleed until she was drifting and empty. She took a deep breath, held it. She could do this. She'd faced down Death himself; what was Famine compared with Death?

"None of us is on *his* level," said Famine.

Missy blinked, nonplussed. Death had also read her mind, so Famine's doing it now was less impressive than it was annoying.

And just like that, Missy's dead face slipped into place, affixing itself to her features seamlessly. "He has manners, at least," she said, her voice tinged with frost. "He doesn't insult people, or attack them."

"Is that what you think? How charming." Beneath the wide brim of her black hat, Famine's eyes glinted, knifelike. "That was hardly an attack. More like a test. You passed, albeit with assistance. Still. Congratulations."

Missy narrowed her eyes.

"As for your other point," Famine said, "I don't make rudeness a habit with my colleagues. But you and I, we go way back. Oh, not you personally, girl," Famine added, contempt coating her words molasses-thick. "You're just the latest skin. And damaged skin, at that."

Cutterslut, one of the Matts whispered.

Missy ground her teeth and told the memory of Matt to go to hell.

"Yes," said the Black Rider, "Famine and War have a history of conflict. Which, I suppose, is rather appropriate, considering your role. But that doesn't make it any more tolerable. The Four must be in balance."

"The Four," Missy repeated slowly.

"The Horsemen, girl. Famine, Pestilence, War, Death. We are the Riders of the Apocalypse."

Thou art War. Thou art the Red Rider of the Apocalypse.

Oh. Right.

Missy toyed with the notion that she was insane. But no—everything that had happened, that was happening now, felt too real for her to simply dismiss as madness. Unbidden, she remembered the feeling of Death's hand as he stroked her cheek, as intimate as frostbite. Yes, that had been real.

Much too real.

This is why I've always liked you, Death said. *You're saucy.*

She shivered, both from the memory and from Famine's words. No matter how crazy it was, she, Melissa Miller, was War—the latest of who knew how many. And, apparently, along with a warhorse and weapon, the role came with baggage. She eyed Famine, who lowered her gloved hand. The bronze set of scales vanished—poof, all gone.

Being a Horseman, Missy decided, meant magic tricks without the sleight of hand normally required. She could see it now: WAR THE MAGICIAN, TUESDAYS AND THURSDAYS STARTING AT FIVE, WITH A SPECIAL APPEARANCE BY FAMINE.

The Black Rider let out a soft laugh. "I may see the wisdom in his choosing one so young to wield the Sword. You're not yet so inflexible."

"I have no idea what you're talking about."

"That's more like it. War tends to be close-minded." Famine sniffed, loudly. "And a bully."

Affronted, Missy replied, "I'm no bully."

"Oh? So the way you forced all those children to experience

anger and terror just moments ago, that was out of the goodness of your heart? Perhaps you were teaching them a life lesson?"

Missy opened her mouth to tell Famine she was crazy . . . but then she remembered the fights that had broken out in Kevin's house, the catcalls and snarls, the bursts of violence erupting like fireworks. Blood drained from her face as Famine's words hit home. Sucker-punched, she said, "No, I wouldn't. I *couldn't*."

"You could and you did," Famine said lightly. "We can call it a learning curve, if that makes you feel better."

Missy sagged against Ares. Oh, God—was it true? Had she been the cause of all of the fighting? Of all that anger?

"Of course it's true," said Famine. "I have no need to lie to you."

Her dead face slipped. Missy, floundering, looked up at Famine and struck blindly. "You're saying all this just to hurt me."

"Well, that too," Famine acknowledged. "I despise you. Your pain is my pleasure. And the truth, as they say, hurts."

Missy tried to let the words wash over her and past her, but they had found the gaps between her dead face and her flesh, and they burrowed deep. Her voice cracking, she asked, "Why?"

"The last time we met, girl, I killed you."

Missy's mouth gaped open, but she couldn't think of a damn thing to say.

"It wasn't personal," Famine added. "You were trying to kill *me*. That, in retrospect, probably *was* personal on your part. The time before that, you *did* kill me." In the shadows of her face, her eyes glittered. "As I said, we have a history, you and I."

Missy remembered the sudden boneless weight of Graygirl going limp in her arms. The world shifted beneath her feet. Clinging to Ares, she cried out, "But *why?*"

"You house the very spirit of aggression, and you ask *me* why you raised your Sword high in slaughter?" Famine shook her head. "Your reaction is amusing, but it's also childish. For all that you are a girl, you're also War. Take responsibility for your actions."

A red tide crashed over Missy, tinting her world in shades of blood. She opened her mouth, but it was War who spoke. "I OWN WHAT I DO, BLACK, MORE THAN ANY OF YOU OTHERS."

Famine smiled thinly. "Ah, there you are. I was wondering when you'd show up."

"EVEN THE PALE RIDER, FOR ALL OF HIS POWER, HAS A ROMANTIC NOTION OF HIS ROLE." War snorted. "WE'RE NO STRUGGLING HEROES, NO CRUSADERS OF JUSTICE. WE ARE THE HARBINGERS OF THE APOCALYPSE."

Missy snapped her mouth closed. No, no—that wasn't her!

"But it is," Famine said. "You're no different than the other Wars before you."

Missy shuddered, wanting to tell the thin woman with her face of shadow that she was wrong, that the words that had spewed from Missy's mouth weren't hers. But War had wrapped its arms around her in thick bands and refused to let her go.

YOU CANNOT FIGHT ME, War told Missy, the voice soothing, numbing. Missy felt her body relax—and she panicked. This wasn't the gentle euphoria she felt after cutting a forearm or the tender flesh of her inner thigh; it was an insistent pull, slowly bleeding her will.

"No," she whispered.

The red voice—the Sword's voice—purred in her mind: *YES.*

"No," she said again, stronger this time. "That's not me. I won't let that be me."

"You're War," the Black Rider said with a shrug. "There is nothing else to you."

Laughter, in her mind, in her memory, as Adam jeered at her, called her a freak.

Missy snapped her head up to stare at the black-clad woman. "How *dare* you," she said, rage sharpening her words so that they sliced the air between the two Riders. "You look at me and label me and dismiss me. But there's more to me than what you see," she said, her voice rising. "I'm deeper than any preconceived notion you have of me. You think you know me," Melissa Miller shouted to the heavens, "think you understand everything about me, but you have no idea who I am!"

Her words echoed in the still air between them.

The Sword clanged once, shrilly, then was silent. Missy still felt its presence in the back of her mind—a red coal, ready to be stoked into a roaring fire. But for now, it was quiet. A small victory.

Something shone behind Famine's black gaze, darkly, like pearls dipped in oil. For a moment, she seemed not a creature of phenomenal power but instead a woman whose skin was stretched too tightly over her face, as if she were constantly biting back a scream. "Balance," the Black Rider said softly, perhaps to herself. "And where will you choose to plant your feet, girl?"

Missy held her gaze and said nothing.

"You say there's more to you than the Sword," Famine said. "Prove it. I'll measure your words against your actions, and from that I will determine your worth."

"I don't give a damn what you think of me," Missy growled.

"That's a lie. And it doesn't matter." Famine nudged her steed with her heels, and the horse slowly turned away. "I'll be watching you, girl. Do your job. Do it to the best of your ability. And perhaps I will apologize to you, should you show me there's more to you than your urge to bring humanity to its knees."

Missy heard the unspoken promise of what Famine would do should Missy not prove herself. "Tell me," she said, tamping down her anger. "Instead of threatening me, tell me: what am I supposed to do?"

Famine looked over her shoulder at Missy. If there was a hint of emotion on her face, it was shrouded by the wide brim of her hat. "Learn on the job, same as the rest of us. And pray you don't tip the balance against you."

The woman in black kicked her heels, and then she and her steed were gone.

Missy stared at the spot where they had been, her thoughts swirling colors of red and black. The anger slowly leeched away, leaving her empty, drained. She was exhausted down to her bones.

"I want to go home," she said to no one in particular. She wanted her bed, her pillow, her room. She wanted life to make sense again, even if it was just for the nothingness of sleep.

Ares let out a nicker. She turned to see the warhorse kneeling so that she could pull herself up.

"Thank you," she murmured once she was on its back, already half asleep.

||||||

The horse said nothing. Even if it could, it wouldn't tell its mistress that what she had done twice now, in the space of a few minutes, its former Riders had never done throughout their entire tenure: thanked the steed for its service.

Some truths were best treasured alone.

||||||

Missy was only half surprised to see Death waiting in her front yard. She was, however, completely surprised to find him spotlighted by the full moon as he sang and played an acoustic guitar.

Seated on Ares' back, Missy settled into the saddle and closed her eyes, listening. A longtime Nirvana fan, she could easily imagine the drums and accordion accompanying Death, but the music he was making didn't need such trappings for it to sound complete. The guitar playing was good, yes, but his voice . . . ah, his voice captivated her: overflowing with melancholy, suffused with bitter knowledge, his voice told her that he understood her, that he could have *been* her. As he sang the chorus, Missy heard longing coloring the words, the risk of hope underlining the intent. Death sang, and Missy heard herself in the song.

"Don't expect me to die," sang Death, "for thee."

Perhaps the song was supposed to be ironic. Or not. Missy was too exhausted to make sense of possible hidden messages wrapped in lyrics, to search for conspiracies within melodies. So instead she merely listened, and felt, and when the final note faded, she was all the sadder for its absence.

"You're not him," she said, "are you?"

Death, seated cross-legged on the front stoop, said nothing, but his eyes were filled with mischief as he regarded her.

"You look like him," Missy said. "You sing like him. But are you him?"

He smiled serenely. "What do you think?"

Missy was too tired to think, so she didn't give him an answer as she slid off of Ares. The horse bowed its head, and with a teeth-rattling whinny, it leapt into the sky and cometed away. Missy blinked stupidly at the space where the steed had been. "Guess I don't have to rub it down or stable it."

"Guess you don't."

She looked at Death as he opened a knapsack and stuffed the guitar into it. When he latched the bag, it was impossible to tell there was a full-size guitar inside. Physics and the supernatural, Missy decided, didn't play nicely together.

Death stood and stretched, giving a small "Ahhh" as something popped in his back. He slouched his way toward his waiting steed. The pale horse nickered, and Death scratched behind its ears before he attached his knapsack to the large saddle.

For all that he was Death, he seemed so very human, from the hunch of his shoulders to the light stubble along his jaw. Missy bit her lip, debating whether to ask, and finally she just blurted it out: "Is Death a voice in your head?"

He glanced over his shoulder at her. His blond hair caught the moonlight even as the wind kissed it, transformed it into a fuzzy halo. "You mean, do I talk to myself?"

"No. Are you *you*," she said, gesturing to him, "and the thing that makes you Death is a voice in your head, talking to you, telling you to do things?" God, she sounded insane.

He held her gaze for a small slice of forever before he spoke. "Why do you ask?"

She didn't want to tell him, but looking into those eyes, she had no choice but to reveal the truth, for all that it could damn her. "Because the Sword is in my head, and it's making me say things I don't mean. It made me do things tonight." Suddenly cold, she rubbed her arms. "Bad things."

"Oh?"

She swallowed thickly and turned away, unwilling to admit what she had done. She wondered if the boy who'd been thrown down the stairs was all right.

"Broken collarbone," Death said. "He won't be good for the baseball team this year."

Missy cringed.

"Could have been worse," he said cheerfully. "Could have been his neck."

That didn't make her feel any better. "It's the Sword," she said, her words coming too fast. "The Sword is in my head, and it sounds so good and right, but the things it says are wrong."

"Wrong?"

"Hurting people is wrong! Getting them to fight and hurt each other is wrong!" Why did she even have to explain that? Wasn't that obvious?

"Aggression is a natural part of human life," said Death. "All the way back to Cain bashing Abel's brains in, all because of whose sacrifice was better. War is in your nature."

"That doesn't make it right." Tears stung her eyes, and she scrubbed angrily at her face. "This thing I am, that you made me when you gave me the Sword—it's evil!"

She wasn't looking at Death, but she could hear the smile in his voice as he asked, "Why do you say that?"

"I'm a Horseman of the Apocalypse," she snarled. "That's

not something you put into the rainbows-and-sunshine column of life!"

"See, you're letting the whole 'Apocalypse' thing taint your opinion." He chuckled softly, and Missy felt his breath on her neck. "It's just a word."

She clenched her teeth to keep from shouting, but she couldn't clamp down on her anger. "It's the end of everything."

"It's a *word*, Melissa Miller," Death whispered in her ear. "Nothing more. Nothing less. Words have power. But so do actions."

"I'm War," she said, her voice breaking. "War is nothing but tragedy."

A cold hand touched her chin, nudged her until she was facing him once more. His face was calm, but his eyes were alight with blue fire. "War can be a tragedy, certainly," he said quietly. "But you could be something more."

She looked at him through her tears, wanting to believe him, positive he was wrong.

"One thing about being as old as I am," he said. "I'm rarely wrong."

She didn't know how to respond. She didn't know why he hadn't removed his hand from her chin. And she didn't know what she was supposed to do next.

"It's late," said Death. "You've been through a lot today, and that was all before you accepted the package I offered you. Go to bed. Sleep and dream. Tomorrow may bring a fresh perspective."

She squeezed her eyes shut, but images of the night's events splattered her mind in red and black. She'd been humiliated; she'd showered people with her fury. She whispered, "And if it doesn't?"

"We can talk about that, should that come to pass." Missy felt his hand stroke her cheek lightly, and then it dropped away. He said, "I bid thee a good night."

By the time Missy opened her eyes, Death was long gone. Her front door stood open, and the porch light was on. It occurred to her that Death, among other things, was a gentleman.

She didn't deserve a gentleman in her life.

Missy went inside and shut the door. She turned off the porch light and leaned heavily against the front door, suddenly and crushingly tired. She could sleep for a month and it wouldn't be enough.

She could sleep forever and it wouldn't be enough.

She barely made it up the stairs. In a fog, she stumbled to the bathroom and did her business and washed her hands and splashed water on her face, smearing her makeup without removing it. She didn't recognize the girl staring back at her from the mirror.

War can be a tragedy, certainly. But you could be something more.

She let out a bitter laugh. Something more than a teenage tragedy? She couldn't handle anything—not school, not Adam, not her life. Not her blade. Not the Sword. She'd hurt people tonight and hadn't even known it. She was a screwup. She didn't deserve to be War, didn't deserve to be anything other than a potential statistic.

Exhausted and heartsick, Missy went to bed. Tears glued her mascaraed lashes to her face, and her leftover red lipstick stained her pillow with bloody kisses.

She dreamed of a dead rock star whose music shredded her heart and scattered the pieces to the wind.

SATURDAY

Missy woke up to an insistent pounding in either her ears or her head. She skimmed the surface of consciousness and was about to plummet back down to the depths of sleep when her father's voice called out: "Melissa! Get up! Your soccer game's in one hour!" This was punctuated by three machine-gun knocks on the bedroom door, each one loud enough to make Missy's teeth vibrate. From elsewhere in the house, her mother chided him for banging on the door.

"I'm up," Missy replied, which really was closer to a very muffled "Mmmmp." But her father got the message. Missy heard her dad's footfalls fade as he went downstairs, God willing, to put up some coffee. Like him, Missy appreciated caffeine, but on a morning like this, it was going to be as necessary as breathing; she was so exhausted, she was lucky she knew her own name.

Thou art War.

God, she had such weird dreams. That she'd even gone to Kevin's party was crazy all by itself—Missy didn't do parties—but then actually hooking up with Adam? And then getting humiliated by him? That was the stuff of nightmares.

And that was before she'd met Death. Who, if she was remembering this right, was a combination of scary and sexy, with a liberal dose of alternative rock god sprinkled in for good measure. She smiled, thinking of his voice—so raw and aching with emotion. Death the musician. She loved Nirvana, but Death as Kurt Cobain? That was pushing it.

And then the dream had gotten *really* weird.

Whatever. She could psychoanalyze herself later. Right now she had to get her butt out of bed and get ready for the game. *The* game, capital *T;* she was finally going to start as goalkeeper. Her smile pulled into a fierce grin. *Finally.*

She scraped away the remnants of last night's mascara and pried her eyes open. It took them a few moments to focus, and she blinked a few times to clear away the fuzz. Why hadn't she washed off her makeup last night? And . . . had she gone to bed wearing her bra?

Forget the bra—she'd crashed out wearing last night's outfit.

She frowned down at her stockings, gently ran her hands over the slashed material covering her thighs. This was the outfit from her dream, the one she'd worn to the party.

Snapshots of memories, flashing one after the other in full color, one, two, three: One, Adam kissing her smoothly and Missy's body remembering how good it was when he touched her. Two, Adam telling her he wanted her, wanted to really see her, all of her.

Three, Missy posing on the bed, her scars on display, and Adam betraying her so completely.

Oh, God.

She squeezed her eyes shut and curled up into a ball. It all happened—she knew it, deep in her bones. Adam had made a fool of her in front of everyone, and she'd fled into the night to escape her life.

She was dead.

The balloon in her chest expanded suddenly, flattening her

heart and making it impossible to breathe. Blood roared in her ears; her scars pounded to a chant of *Freak, freak, freak.*

She was damaged goods; she was broken.

Freak.

She needed the blade. She needed to open her flesh and free her veins and stain her skin. She had to cut and cut and cut, get the badness out, slice away the tatters of her life until the balloon popped and she could breathe again. The razor would smooth the jagged pieces and kiss it all away. There was no redemption other than through blood.

A pounding at the door: "Melissa! Let's go!"

The balloon shrank and she took a labored breath; the horror receded and she could see beyond the blade. Her life was in ruins, but she still had her soccer game. For now, it was enough; for now, she would live for the joy of battle in cleats and shin guards, for the savage fury of stealing the other team's victory. She could do that.

Thou art War.

She could do that, she told herself again, and she forced herself to sit up. She felt like a piece of gum stuck on the bottom of a shoe—filthy, sticky, and flat. A headache pulsed behind her eyes. Her wrists and thighs and belly throbbed as if her razor had done its work, but there was no quiet bliss to be found this morning. She stared hard at the carpet by the closet, looking for traces of bloodstains. But the carpet was clean, as if her slow crawl to the closet had never happened.

Shaking, she stripped off her clothing, her bra, her stockings. No panties. Right; her underwear and her boots had been confiscated, hadn't they? Just more pieces of her life carved away. She stood in front of the full-length mirror on the back of her door and stared at herself, at the road map of scars and cuts and razor-prints, and through her crusted makeup she began to cry, softly, letting out the horror the only way she could.

In the bathroom, she relieved herself, then scrubbed her face and hands with painfully hot water, leaving her flesh battered and raw. She scoured her teeth until they gleamed—bones nestled in a bed of bleeding gums.

Missy dressed silently, cotton underwear and a sports bra and knee-length soccer socks and baggy shorts. Her red uniform top—with the long sleeves of a goalkeeper—hid her sins from casual eyes. She threw her shin guards and gloves and cleats into her duffle bag, weapons at the ready. She pulled back her hair into a topknot, the ends trailing behind her like the plume on a helmet.

She stared at herself in the mirror again, took in the warrior in red that stared back at her.

"I am War," she said quietly.

She thought she heard Death reply, "Rock on." But of course, there was no one else in her room; even the ghost of Graygirl was silent.

Missy jogged downstairs and dashed into the kitchen. No time for breakfast proper, but a few sips of coffee, light and sweet, was next on her agenda. Besides, there was milk in the half-and-half, so she was getting caffeine *and* protein.

Her father tapped his watch as she grabbed a mug. "Five minutes," he said.

"You coming to the game?"

He actually managed to look apologetic. Missy wanted to tell him not to bother; they'd all had years to perfect this particular routine. By now she knew the gestures along with the words, the choreography that worked with the script. First the "I Wish," then the "Difficult and Counting," followed with a plastic "Next." For her part, she kept her face carefully neutral, like Switzerland—not her dead face, never that for her father or mother, but a delicately painted mask of understanding.

"I wish I could, Missy." Between her nickname and his hand clapping her shoulder in parental affection, her father was showing her how sincere he was. "But work's been difficult, and the CEO's counting on me to have the next round of specs nailed down for her on Monday, so I have to go in today. Next game, okay?" This last said with a smile pulled out of commercials and magazines. It was a good smile, full of teeth and empty promise.

Missy's turn. She kept her own smile small and guarded— not an "aw, shucks" and definitely not a "screw you" but somewhere in the middle. It was a smile that said she knew how the world worked and she didn't like it, but she accepted it. "Next game," she said, knowing that would never happen.

He clapped her shoulder again, then grabbed her duffle bag to load it into the car—his version of a mea culpa. The door to the garage banged closed, and Missy loosened her mask enough for her smile to slip free. By now she knew better than to expect her dad, or her mom, to attend any of her games; there was always something else going on, usually work-related, that her folks had to tackle. But part of her had quietly hoped that for this game, her first ever as starting goalkeeper, one of them would make an exception.

A buzzing laughter, like hornets. THEY'RE SHEEP.

Missy's knuckles whitened around her mug handle. Her parents weren't sheep.

OF COURSE THEY ARE. THEY DO WHAT THEY'RE TOLD AND NOTH-ING MORE. WORK HARD. MAKE MONEY. DON'T THINK. More laughter as the hornets swarmed. SHEEP, THE BOTH OF THEM, MEANT TO BE LED AND SHORN, AND SOMETIMES BLED.

Missy bit down on her lip, hard. The momentary sting was enough to quell the voice, to give War a taste of blood. Her lip throbbing, she poured herself a cup of coffee. She was stirring in the sugar when Sue walked into the kitchen, yawning. She saw Missy and froze, mid-yawn, caught in surprise.

Sue looked so *stupid*. The thought made Missy grin.

For a long moment, Sue looked at Missy, taking in everything from her soccer uniform to her hair to the mug in her hand. Sue's gaze crept over Missy's face, latched on to Missy's eyes. Something passed behind Sue's face—liquid emotion, all bittersweet chocolate and flat soda. The moment passed, and Sue shut down until her face was as plastic as their father's smile. Her mouth pressed into a thin white line, she glided past Missy to get a glass from the cabinet, her slippers whispering against the linoleum floor.

Well, someone was in a *mood*.

Missy chuckled, then took a sip of coffee. The hot liquid stung as it glided over her sore lip and sensitive gums, but she relished the pain. With one sip, she proved herself alive and grounded. The pain was better than the jolt of caffeine.

Sue glared at her, and Missy was amused by the cold fury in that gaze. When Sue didn't say anything, Missy asked, "Something wrong?"

"You selfish bitch." Sue's words were the hiss of teakettle steam, boiling hot. "You never think about anyone but yourself, do you?"

"I'm thinking about you right now, sis. Want to know what I'm thinking? First word rhymes with *duck*."

Sue slammed her glass on the counter and walked up to Missy, got right in her face. She snarled, "You think that your life's so damn hard that you have to throw it away? Do you have any idea what that would do to Mom and Dad? Do you even care?"

Missy tried to make sense of Sue's words and failed. In lieu of comprehension, she went with irritation. "The hell are you talking about?"

"This." Sue grabbed Missy's arm and yanked back the sleeve. Scars, white and pink and scabbed and ugly and fine and intricate and so very red, crisscrossed Missy's exposed flesh.

Caught. Missy was caught. Again.

She slapped her dead face on, its edges askew, and though her heartbeat careened crazily in her chest, her face was marble perfection—impassive, cold, unconcerned.

"This," Sue repeated, softer. "For God's sake, Missy. What are you *doing*?"

That couldn't be sympathy in Sue's voice. Sue didn't give a damn about Missy—she'd said as much ever since the school year started and Sue discovered that Missy was at the wrong end of the Socially Acceptable spectrum. Missy pulled away, slopping coffee onto the floor.

"I'm not suicidal," Missy said, "if that's what you're afraid of."

"Then what's that all over your arm? A messed-up tattoo?"

Irritation bled into anger. Missy shoved her sleeve back into place. "How'd you find out? You spying on me? Reading my diary?" Not that she had a diary, but still.

"The hundreds of texts and emails I got were a big clue." Sue narrowed her eyes. "Some party last night, huh?"

Missy felt the blood drain from her face. Trusting Adam had reduced her to nothing more than fodder for teen paparazzi greed and gossip. She'd known it would happen; one didn't emerge from the flash of cell phone cameras unscathed. But knowing and *knowing* were two different things. Sickened, she took a sip of coffee, trying for normal and failing. Even with all the sugar and cream, it was bitter.

"You look me in the eye," Sue said, "and you tell me you're not trying to kill yourself."

Missy closed her eyes. Sue didn't understand.

No one understood.

This was the moment. She could tell her sister about the pressure in her chest, about the way everything expanded into Too Much and threatened to drag her under. She could tell her that she turned to the blade because she wanted to live and sometimes pain was the only thing that kept her alive. She could tell her that she was terrified of things she couldn't even begin to name, that friends could be fickle and lovers could be false. She could try to explain all of that and more, and maybe her sister would understand.

But trust was as fragile and cutting as a crystal sword. Missy had bled too much already . . . and she had one Sword too many.

So she carefully rebuilt the glass jar of her heart, fusing the shards into place until the bottle was perfect. She shoved in the feelings before they suffocated her: the embarrassment of being caught; the gratitude for Sue actually caring, even a little; the fear of what happened next; and the rage, above all else—rage over not being in control of her own life, over being manipulated for other people's amusement, over the sheer unfairness of it all. She pushed it all into the glass jar and sealed it tight, and then she opened her eyes and gently put down her mug. She was flat; she was empty. She had her dead face and her glass jar. Nothing could affect her anymore. She wouldn't let anything, anyone in. The world could rot and she wouldn't care.

She wouldn't care.

Looking her sister in the eye, she said, "I'm not trying to kill myself."

Silence, thick and cloying, finally broken by the sound of Sue's teeth grinding, grinding. "You think you're making a *statement*, maybe?" Sue hissed. "Well, your statement brands me too. Because this morning, all I am is the sister of a suicidal wannabe emo *freak*."

Those words carved Missy's flesh as surely as her razor had ever done.

Sue blew out a ragged breath. "You know, I didn't believe them when I heard you were a cutter. I thought it was just Adam being a loser ex-boyfriend, being vicious just because. People exaggerate, I thought. Makes a better story. People lie for points. But it was *all true*. You take a knife to your skin." She sneered, her lip curling in derision. "You're a sick excuse of a sister. I'm embarrassed to know you."

Of course, that was when their father walked in. Missy stiffened, uncertain how much he had heard—and unsure whether Sue would keep their conversation private. Their father frowned at the two girls. "Enough with the fighting," he said. "You're sisters. Hug and make up. Then let's go, Missy. You're running late."

Sue grinned, bright enough to blind. She opened her arms wide, ever the good daughter.

Missy smiled, tight as piano wire. She hugged her sister, and Sue wrapped her arms around her.

"Say anything," Missy whispered in Sue's ear, "and you're dead."

Sue's breath on her neck. "Like I'd even bother."

They pulled apart as if on cue. Missy saw the brittleness behind Sue's fake grin, how it looked like she was trying to keep herself from screaming. Her sister was genuinely upset—but whether it was for Missy or because of Missy, Missy couldn't say.

Troubled, Missy adjusted her dead face, tightened the stopper on the glass jar, then followed her father out the door.

||||||

Breathing hard, Missy palmed her hair out of her eyes. She cursed herself yet again for forgetting a headband. She cursed herself for letting the ball get through that one time. Most of all, she cursed herself for being tired. She was sixteen. She was immortal. She wasn't supposed to be tired, not after only seventy-five minutes of game time.

Okay, so maybe she was supposed to be tired. Still. The last thing she wanted was for the coach to decide she wasn't a starter. So she mentally slapped herself, focused on the game, and bobbed back and forth in a ready position as the opposing team passed the ball closer and closer. *Here it comes, midfield to right forward, back to midfield and a fakeout to left before passing back to right forward, and then the attack on the goal.* Missy danced on the line, running side to side and biting back the urge to shout at her teammate Trudy to get her thumb out of her ass and block the kick. If this were war, Trudy would be the wide-eyed soldier who didn't duck to avoid the shrapnel.

Forget Trudy, Missy told herself. *Watch the legs, watch the hips, watch the eyes.*

A blur of footwork, and the forward left Trudy behind as she drove the ball to the net.

Don't let it through.

The striker was looking hard at Missy's left, even as she moved toward her right. Missy launched herself out of the box to her left just as the other girl cannoned the shot. Missy mistimed it, but she saved the goal with a parrying kick that blasted the soccer ball down the field. She landed hard on her shoulder, grunting from the impact.

Get up get up get up.

Missy pulled herself to her feet and saw Jenna working the ball center left. The opposing striker was making Jenna sweat, and Missy read the girl's body language easily. "She's going to come your way," she shouted to Trudy.

Trudy blatantly ignored her, as she had the entire game. As most of her teammates had the entire game.

THEIR BLOOD IS AS RED AS ANYONE ELSE'S.

That thought hadn't come from Missy.

She gritted her teeth and shimmied left and right as the ball escaped Jenna. Down came the striker, with Trudy nipping at her heels. The forward cut right, and Missy pounced, stealing the ball. She threw it away, wiped sweat from her eyes, and glanced at Trudy as she got back inside the box.

Nothing. It was like Missy didn't exist.

Missy told herself it didn't matter. She told herself it didn't bother her. She told herself other things, too, every single one of them a lie.

The ball stayed downfield as Missy's team attacked. Successfully, rah. Now all they had to do was prevent the other team from scoring in the last two minutes of game time.

No pressure.

Missy shuffled side to side, her eyes on the field as she moved. She watched Jenna dribble the ball away from the opposing striker, watched as the striker wove her way from behind Jenna and snagged her leg in front of the girl, kicking the ball away and tripping Jenna beautifully. Watched Jenna hit the ground and glare at the striker, who was already moving away.

WEAK, War thought. And Missy agreed. Glaring at the enemy didn't stop them. Jenna should have at least fallen on the other girl, or flailed out with her arms to accidentally clip the girl's face. If you go down in battle, you take your opponent with you.

The ball rocketed down the field, and Missy lunged out of the box. She scooped up the ball just as the striker slammed into her, knocking the ball free. Missy made a desperate grab and missed—but Trudy was there, kicking the ball well away from the goal.

And the whistle blew. Game over.

Missy pumped her fist in the air, euphoric from the victory. She lined up with the others to do the traditional "good game" hand slapping, which was all nonsense, of course—it wasn't about playing well, win or lose. The only good game was a game you won, period. But Missy could afford to be magnanimous—after all, they'd won.

A minute later, it was over. The other team left to lick their wounds, and the coach gave Missy and the girls a post-game talk that Missy barely heard. Bella, benched for the whole game, high-fived Missy and ran down all of the various plays she'd done right as well as those she needed to do better for the next game. "For your first time," Bella said, grinning, "not bad at all."

High praise from Bella. Missy soaked it up and asked for seconds.

War, who appreciated victory above all else, basked.

All that was left was changing out of their game clothes, then would come the victory sundaes at the ice cream shop. Bella went ahead to book enough tables for sixteen. The team broke away from Missy as the girls grouped their way to the locker room. She trailed after them, still giddy, the Sword humming pleasantly in her head.

But in the locker room, everything changed.

"Wonder how that happened," Jenna said, giggling at Missy's duffle bag on the floor, stinking of urine.

"Guess the toilet was backed up," said Trudy.

Missy stared in mute fury at her soaked bag. Her wallet, her shoes, her change of clothes—all were ruined.

"Sorry you can't come with us," said Jenna, sounding not at all sorry.

"Much better for you to go home and do your laundry," Trudy added.

They'd pissed on her things just to disinvite her from the ice cream hangout. They hadn't even had the courage to tell her to her face.

"Besides," said Jenna, "we wouldn't want you to bleed over all the ice cream."

Laughter, girlish and cruel, filled the locker room.

Missy clenched her fist so hard, it shook.

KILL THEM, War whispered gleefully. *KILL THEM ALL.*

She could. She could lose herself in the Red and let War out to play. She could brandish her Sword and show them all what power truly was. She could destroy them so easily.

DO IT.

She could baptize them in blood.

DO IT!

She could sing to them the gospel of pain.

DO IT!

Yes, she could do it. She *should* do it. With a thought, the Sword would appear in her hand and she would slaughter them all. Their bodies would crumple, lifeless, their blood spatter slick and shining, crimson petals on the locker room floor. She would turn their death into art.

Missy smiled, slowly, letting it bloom poisonously sweet as she looked first at Jenna, then at Trudy. She didn't know what they saw on her face, but Trudy paled and Jenna narrowed her eyes.

"You have something to say?" Jenna demanded.

Missy heard the girl's scorn, felt her anger. Tasted her fear. That made Missy grin wider. Jenna only *thought* she was afraid. She didn't know what terror was, not really.

Missy could teach her.

She could teach her so very much.

KILL THEM ALL!

Just before she could call her Sword and massacre her teammates, she heard a cold voice whisper: *Control.*

Clinging to that word—both a command for humanity and a plea for sanity—Missy walked away. The locker room door banged shut behind her, cutting off the sound of nervous, jeering laughter.

WEAK, War scolded. *YOU'RE WEAK. DAMAGED SKIN, AS THE BLACK RIDER SAID. NOTHING MORE.*

Snarling, Missy finally drew her Sword. Its weight felt so very good in her gloved hand, so very right. She thought of her steed, and Ares appeared in a burst of red, falling from the sky like a comet.

"I'm supposed to be War," she told the horse. "So let's see some war."

Ares bowed, and Missy vaulted up. Sword in one hand, reins in the other, she howled as Ares took to the sky.

Beneath them, the world trembled.

CHAPTER 10

They cut a path through the sky, the Sword blazing in Missy's hand as the steed's hooves thundered like cannon fire. All who beheld the Red Rider that day thought they glimpsed a falling star, and to a person they thought of shattered glass and wind-swept debris, of carnage and steel. And when those people came into contact with others that day, they fought, or loved, or played with more passion than they had since they took their first bloody, newborn breaths—which, long ago, had been heralded by a slap.

Life's first lesson: life itself is violent. Happy birthday.

Melissa Miller understood violence intimately. She wanted nothing more than to share that knowledge with everyone she came across. Visions of murder twinkling darkly behind her eyes, she rode, ready to tear the world asunder.

Below, land streaked by in vicious strips of red. From the smallest flyspeck village to the largest industrialized city, emotions dotted the land like fireflies at night. Missy sensed them all and shredded them, leaving tatters of fear and fury to drift in her wake. The sleeping wrestled with nightmares; those awake blinked through red-tinted glass and gave in to their primal urges—food, fun, and fighting, all of it unrestrained. The police and EMTs would be busy well into the next day.

Missy thought it nothing more than her flexing her power. War merely liked to play with her toys.

Ares slowed, and the luminescent reds slowly gave way to solid browns stained with gold, to stubborn mountains splitting the ground in snaggletoothed grins and sun-ravaged earth pounded flat from the desert heat. Speckled through the barren stretch of land were tents—thousands and thousands of them, arranged in clusters, with some areas marked by blue plastic tarp held in place by sticks and stones.

Scattered among the tents were people, easily a quarter million of them, wearing clothing stained by dirt and sweat and sun: adults sitting in groups, squatting over dust and rocks, moving listlessly, tying down tent flaps, waiting in impossibly long lines with pans in their hands and straw hats on their heads; children playing, filled with energy fueled by youth and imagination, chatting, drawing pictures in the sand and on paper; babies on their mother's hip, little more than appendages.

Missy saw them all from her perch up on high, and she swallowed thickly, tasting dust and despair. She had envisioned guns and tanks, battles raging to blockbuster movie soundtracks. She had thought longingly of surface-to-air missiles and smart planes and nuclear bombs—long-range weapons, as powerful as they were efficient killing machines. Video game violence, with video game consequences.

She hadn't put faces to war.

They are all the same, War murmured. *They flee when they hear the report of gunfire in their backyards, taking their families and the clothing on their backs as they run like rats in the night.*

Children, Missy thought numbly. *Babies.*

War barked laughter, the *rat-a-tat* of a machine gun. *Even nine year olds can throw grenades.*

The red steed whinnied as it spiraled down—a flying horse version of a Fasten Seatbelts sign. Missy, frowning at the desert scene, held tight to reins and Sword, and she told herself that the building nausea in her belly was due to the sudden landing. She sat atop Ares and breathed in the smell of urine and feces; the refuse was in neat piles, covered with dirt, but it wasn't enough to bury the stench. Deeper than the toilet odors were the animal aromas of thousands upon thousands of people penned in the open air, their sweat burned away by the sun's merciless heat.

Lightheaded, Missy closed her eyes. That didn't stop the smells, or the sounds of conversation so low and so widespread that they were little more than the buzzing of words, competing with the actual buzzing of flies that riddled the makeshift campground. She heard stray snatches of children's laughter caught in the hot, hot wind. Beyond that, faintly, the inconsistent popping of gunplay echoed in the mountains.

A child's delighted screech made her open her eyes, and she saw a boy—or maybe a girl—kick a ball with a bare, filthy foot. He might have been three years old, and he toddled over the flat expanse of dirt and rocks as he kicked that ball, and he bubbled laughter.

Missy watched the tiny soccer player and her eyes burned. "What is this?" she whispered.

THEIR GOVERNMENT FIGHTS INSURGENT REBELS, War told her.

"Why are they fighting?"

RELIGION. POLITICS. GIVE IT THE NAME YOU WISH, BUT IN THE END, IT'S ALL ABOUT CONTROL. IT'S ALWAYS ABOUT CONTROL.

Missy thought she heard Death chuckle, but he was nowhere to be seen. "These people aren't fighters," she said, watching the little boy kick the soccer ball.

REFUGEES, War sneered. *DISPLACED WHEN THE INSURGENTS FLOODED THEIR VILLAGES AND THEIR GOVERNMENT RETALIATED WITH BOMBS DROPPED FROM PLANES. THE SKIES BELONG TO THEIR LEADERS, BUT THE MOUNTAINS BELONG TO THE REBELS. AND THE GROUND BELONGS TO WHOEVER CAN HOLD IT. REFUGEES MAKE WONDERFUL SHIELDS.*

"Stop it," Missy gritted.

STOP? WHY? THIS IS WHAT PEOPLE DO. THEY FIGHT ONE ANOTHER. THEY DESTROY ONE ANOTHER. THEY WANT WHAT OTHERS HAVE, AND THEY TAKE IT.

Missy thought of Adam, of his casual lies and choreographed betrayal. She felt his hands on her body, heard the cruel glee in his voice as he called her a freak. "That doesn't make it right."

Death's voice, coldly serene: *War is in your nature.*

Ares nickered, perhaps to remind Missy that she was War and thus she had a job to do. Or maybe the red horse just wanted her to get off its back.

Missy sheathed the Sword and slid off of the warhorse, landing on shaky legs. Her cleats bit into the ground, and she slowly found her balance.

Balance, Famine had said to her, smooth as melted chocolate. *And where will you choose to plant your feet, girl?*

A shudder worked through Missy, and she shoved her emotions into the glass jar of her heart. Then she took a deep breath. *I wanted this,* she told herself. *I accepted the Sword.* "Where is this place?"

War told her.

"But . . ." Missy's voice trailed off. She hadn't heard about this particular war, or conflict, or years-long battle, or whatever it was—not in school, not at home, not on television.

MEDIA BLACKOUT, War said with a verbal shrug. *REPORTERS ARE BANNED FROM THE WARZONES.*

Even if this particular war were televised for one's dinner entertainment, Missy thought bitterly as she watched the toddler chase after the ball, she wouldn't have known about it. She wasn't exactly concerned with the events of the world. Missy didn't sign up to save the rainforests, or volunteer to clean up the park, or work in a soup kitchen. She was a sixteen-year-old high school junior, overscheduled and underappreciated and barely able to tread water without feeling like she was about to drown.

She thought of razors and bloody towels, and her breath hitched in her throat.

A group of children rushed past Missy, either playing tag or just running for the simple joy of feeling their bodies move. The adults nearest Missy were talking in hushed voices, in a language she didn't know and yet understood completely. They were speaking of the dwindling supplies.

MORE REFUGEES COME EVERY DAY, War commented idly. *TWO HUNDRED OF THEM, EVERY DAY.*

Missy watched the children play. "What happens when the supplies run out?"

THAT IS NOT MY CONCERN. LET FAMINE HAVE THEM.

A crack ran along the side of the glass jar. "Don't you care?"

WHY SHOULD I? THE BLACK RIDER GETS THEM ANYWAY, said War. *OR POSSIBLY THE WHITE. IT'S ALL THE SAME TO ME.*

The glass jar shattered, and Missy sank to the rocky ground, dizzy and heartsick and disgusted. Near her, a group of children began to argue over who got to sleep on their one mattress that night. Another child stole the toddler's soccer ball, leaving the little boy to wail.

"You'll let them all suffer," she cried, "even the babies—and for what? What possible reason could you have to hurt them so much?"

I DO NOTHING LESS THAN EXPECTED, War said. *AND YOU PEOPLE EXPECT SO VERY MUCH FROM YOUR PAIN. YOU DEMAND SALVATION EVEN AS YOU STEAL FROM THE COLLECTION PLATE.*

Tears gleamed in Missy's eyes. "No."

YOU SEND FOOD AND SUPPLIES TO THE REFUGEES, AND THEN YOU DON'T ALLOW THE DELIVERY TRUCKS THROUGH THE WARZONES. THE FOOD WILL SPOIL, THE SUPPLIES WILL BE SOLD BY THE VICTORS. THE CIVILIANS WILL STARVE, AND SICKEN, AND EVENTUALLY DIE.

War's proclamation settled in to Missy's bones. "That's not true," she insisted, hugging herself tightly and rocking on the desert floor.

IT IS THE WAY OF THINGS. THEY WILL ALL DIE, WHETHER FROM THE BRUTAL SAVAGERY THAT IS UNIQUE TO MAN OR FROM THE ABUNDANCE OF DISEASE OR FROM THE SCARCITY OF SUSTENANCE. War's voice was the murmur of sweet nothings, the heated promise of true love. *THEY WILL ALL DIE. AT LEAST MY WAY, THEY DIE WITH A PURPOSE.*

Missy saw the destruction of the world in neon flashes, burning the backs of her eyes—the end of everything by fire and by ice, by human hand and by nature, by degrees and by one cataclysmic instant that brought the universe itself to its knees. She shook her head as each vision seared her, denying what she saw. "Stop it," she said, her throat raw.

THEY DIE, AND THEN THEY GO TO THE PALE RIDER. A thoughtful pause, and then War said, *AS DO WE ALL, IN THE END.*

Missy shouted, "Stop it!"

DEATH'S ARMS WILL BE THE LAST ONES WE FEEL AROUND US,

HOLDING US CLOSE. HIS KISS WILL BE THE LAST UPON OUR LIPS. OUR BREATH WILL BECOME HIS AS WE GIVE OURSELVES TO HIM.

Missy clutched her hands to her ears and screamed, "STOP IT!"

WAR IS THE HERALD OF DEATH. HE IS OUR GOD. AND YOU ARE HIS HANDMAIDEN, MELISSA MILLER.

Missy climbed to her feet and unsheathed the Sword, a snarl stretching her lips in a parody of a grin. With a defiant cry, she hurled the weapon as far as she could. It arced high in the air, spinning merrily and winking in the desert sun before it disappeared in the mountains. Next to her, Ares snorted, but whether that was due to surprise, amusement, or the dusty air was impossible to know.

Panting, seething, Missy chanted her mantra, the one that had kept her sane for the two months between Graygirl's death and Adam's betrayal: *I don't need the blade. I don't need the blade. I don't.*

In the back of her mind, a kiss of steel: *BUT YOU WILL. AND WHEN YOU TAKE IT UP AGAIN, I WILL BE THERE.*

"Over my dead body," Missy snarled.

"If only it were that easy," a woman said from behind her.

She stiffened as those sickly sweet words hit her, stoking an urge of appetite deep within. Missy slowly turned to face Famine.

CHAPTER 11

The Black Rider stood, shadowlike, stretched tall and thin and woefully dark, even in the light of the desert sun. Farther back, the black horse stood aloof, its white eyes glowing softly.

Missy heard Ares snort its response, felt her steed's fury radiate as if its body were aflame. But her gaze was locked onto the thin figure in black. The wide-brimmed hat hid Famine's face, but Missy saw white teeth flash in a quick smile before it was eaten by shadow.

"No matter how much you run from your responsibility," said Famine, "it has a nasty way of finding you."

"I'm not running," Missy said. "I'm quitting."

"Quitting? You've been on the job an entire day, and it's already too much for you?" Famine sniffed. "I would have thought War was made of sterner stuff."

War was; of that Missy had no doubt. "I'm not War," she said.

"Of course you are. You think just because you throw away your symbol of office that you no longer have an office?" Famine clucked her tongue. "A king without a crown is still a king, even if his empire is only dirt."

Kings and crowns; stuff and nonsense. This was no storybook tale of heroes and legends.

OF BATTLES, War whispered. *OF GLORY.*

No, she wasn't listening to that blazing voice. "The Sword makes me War," Missy said through clenched teeth. "And I threw away the Sword."

"It doesn't, and you did. That changes nothing." Famine took a step closer.

Next to Missy, Ares stomped a hoof and bared its teeth, clearly promising to rip the Black Rider apart if she came within reach. Behind the Black Rider, the black horse merely watched.

Famine smiled thinly at the warhorse. "You see? Your steed defends you. If you were not still War, it would eat you."

Ares flicked its ears, but Missy didn't know if her steed was agreeing with Famine or mocking her. She frowned at the black horse, at the way it simply stood there, taking in the scene as if watching a play—or, considering its Rider, dinner theater. *Famine moves, stage right, delivers her poignant soliloquy. Applause. Fade to black. Pass the salt.* She remembered Ares snapping its teeth at the black horse just last night outside Kevin's house; she remembered how Famine had to murmur to her steed to quiet it.

If the black horse thought Famine were in danger, it would have protected her. Just as Ares had been protecting Missy. She reached over to the warhorse and stroked its neck, tempering it with her touch. For whatever reason Famine had come, it hadn't been to fight—not unless Missy delivered the first blow.

"Now stop your sulking," Famine said, "and do what you're meant to do."

Missy gave the red horse a final pat before she stepped away. She thought of a gray cat, remembered the feeling of soft fur threading around her fingers, remembered hearing a content purr that loosened even the tightest knots in her neck and shoulders. Missy dug her nails into the meat of her palms and was rewarded with eight tiny bites. With pain came clarity, and she said, "What I'm meant to do? You mean encourage people to hurt each other? Kill each other? No thank you."

Famine sighed. "Such a small mind. You used to have such a vibrant imagination, if a bloody one. And you used to come girded for battle. What happened? Laundry day?"

"I had a soccer game."

Famine snorted. "Human things. You've moved past such things, War."

"I told you. I quit."

"You didn't. You merely had a tantrum." The Black Rider smiled, a knife-flash of teeth quickly eaten by the shadows of her face. "Which, as far as that goes, was not nearly as impressive as some of your more spectacular fits of temper. Like that time during the summer of 1945."

Missy's stomach pitched. "You're saying War got mad, so two bombs got dropped on Japan?"

"I'm saying the time for child's play is done. You're War, whether you like it or not. Now accept your role, retrieve your Sword, and get to work."

Sickened by the notion of bombs dropping over a slight to War either imagined or real, Missy shook her head. "No." A million times no.

The Black Rider said nothing for a long moment, and the space was filled with the sounds of a toddler crying over his stolen ball, and of children's screeching laughter—a malicious sound, mocking and cruel. Missy's nostrils stung with the remembered stench of urine, and her ears rang with Jenna's taunt about not bleeding all over the ice cream. Missy clenched her fists and stared murder at the young thieves. They, in turn, began to fight—which ended all too quickly with a bloody nose and a tongue-lashing from an exhausted parent. The toddler kept crying for his lost ball, even when an adult tried to soothe him.

When Famine spoke again, her voice was soft, thoughtful. "The elders here in the refugee camp, they whisper among themselves. They fret over their supplies, over the battlefield that seems closer every day. Over how the world has forgotten them. They wonder if God has turned away."

Missy glanced at the woman in black. Famine's back was to her, her long coattails dancing in the hot wind. "Has he? Turned away?"

"You'd have to ask Death," Famine replied.

Missy thought of the Pale Rider, of a man with bottomless eyes and a crafty smile, and her cheeks burned.

"They're right to worry," said Famine. "At the rate they're going, they have enough food for three days. A week, if the adults give their portions to the children."

Missy kicked the rocky ground. She didn't want to hear this, didn't want to know the death sentence of a quarter million people. "Because the supply trucks aren't being allowed through the warzones," she said sullenly. "I know."

Famine looked over her shoulder at Missy. Beneath the hat's shadow, her eyes shone brightly. "You don't sound happy about it."

Happy? Happy was for birthdays and Disney dwarfs. Missy glared at the Black Rider. "What about this could possibly make me happy?"

"This is your demesne." Famine lifted a gloved hand and motioned to the camp and beyond it, to the mountains that kept the battle away from the refugees. "All of this is because of war. You should be overjoyed."

Missy snarled, "You're sick if you think there's anything enjoyable about any of this."

"Sickness is for Pestilence. I'm merely stating the truth. War thrives on destruction, relishes the sound of despair. This should be mother's milk to you."

"I told you," Missy growled. "I'm not War."

"But you are."

Missy screamed in frustration and impotent fury. "I don't want this! I don't want people to kill each other, to destroy each other for ideology or politics or any reason at all!" She flung her hand toward the refugees. "I don't want any part of this!"

Impassive in the face of Missy's wrath, Famine said, "Then change it."

Just like that: change it. Missy let out a bitter laugh, one that coated her throat like honey. "You keep saying I'm still War. So how can War stop war?"

"You *can't* stop war," Famine replied. "It's human nature. You could no more tell a bird not to fly or a fish not to swim."

"Great," Missy said, defeated. "So no matter what, this happens."

"Of course. If there were no war, there would be no need of a Red Rider."

A Rider in the face of the storm; a Rider to lead the way to destruction. *The end of everything.* Chilled, Missy rubbed her arms. *Apocalypse.*

Death's voice, a cold caress in the desert heat: *It's just a word.*

"I'm not saying we destroy the world," Famine said in a huff. "And I didn't tell you to stop war. I said if you don't want any part of what you see, then *change it.*"

Change. As if the word alone told her what to do.

Words have power, Death had told her. *But so do actions.*

"Don't you see, girl? Balance," said Famine. "It's always about balance. When the scales tip, we're there to right them once more."

Missy stammered, "I-I don't understand."

"Of course not. Because you keep insisting you're not War." Famine walked over to her steed and offered it something from her pocket. As the black horse chewed, she said, "You know, Pestilence quit once. Needed a mental health break, or some such thing. Set aside his crown, and he left." She slid a dark look at Missy. "And in his absence, the Black Death took out most of Europe."

Missy's heart slammed in her chest.

"When the fatalities approached a hundred million, Death went looking for Pestilence, who had been on a beach somewhere, getting a little skin cancer. When Death found him, the two talked. And when they were done, Pestilence got back on his steed and rode again. He couldn't undo the damage that had been done. But he stopped it from spreading any further. That took some time—about five hundred years."

Bile rose in Missy's throat.

"By the nineteenth century, he eradicated the plague from Europe. So many lives lost, all because he had turned away from his responsibility. One wonders," Famine said idly, "with the broad array of nuclear goodies people have today, what would happen if you really were to quit."

Missy commanded herself not to vomit. Sweat popped on her brow, and she swayed, lightheaded, but she forced her nausea to abate. "So I'm trapped."

"Of course not. If you die, then Death would tap someone else to be War. If you really want that," said Famine, "I would be happy to oblige."

She thought of what waited for her back in her life—she was at best a laughingstock, and at worst she was persona non grata, a living pariah with almost two years before she could escape through college and start over. Adam had destroyed her.

YOU GIVE HIM TOO MUCH POWER, War murmured. HE WAS NOTHING MORE THAN A CATALYST.

He couldn't handle her scars. That had been the true cause of everything—the reason she had lost Adam, had pulled away from the few people, such as Erica, who had genuinely cared about her. Missy laughed, the sound a strangled scream. She had cut to keep herself grounded, to make life less overwhelming. She had bled herself again and again so that everything would make sense, so that she could breathe easier. And it had cost her everything.

Her life was nothing but a teenage tragedy.

"*War can be a tragedy, certainly,*" Death said quietly, his eyes alight with blue fire. "*But you could be something more.*"

Remembering his cool touch on her face, Missy stared at the refugee camp, at the displaced people whose lives had been ravaged by war. She stared at them, her thoughts whirling, and an idea took root. It bloomed slowly, and as it unfurled, Missy's hands shook. The thought terrified her—but what scared her even more was the notion of *not* acting on her idea, of shutting herself away while War's version of the Black Death rained down upon the world.

She couldn't quit. And she didn't want to die. That left her only one option.

Missy looked at the children, who were kicking the soccer ball while the toddler continued to cry. She marched over to the small group, snatched the ball, and gave it to the little boy. He laughed in delight and began to kick it. When another child tried to steal it, he bit the girl's arm.

Missy smiled grimly. In her mind, War chortled. WHETHER IT'S A CHILD'S TOY OR A NATION'S OIL, IT'S ALL THE SAME, the Red Rider said. YOU FIGHT FOR WHAT YOU WANT. AGGRESSION. IT'S THE SPICE OF LIFE.

War was right: people had to fight for what they wanted. It was a matter of degree, Missy decided. Or maybe balance, as Famine had said—strength matched with temperance.

No, she thought. *Not balance. Control.*

IT'S ALWAYS ABOUT CONTROL, War agreed merrily.

Missy understood the need for control. She imagined razor-sharp kisses along her skin, the sting of blood meeting air, the euphoria of calmness after a cut.

She couldn't stop war, according to Famine. But she could give something to these people, and to the people beyond the mountains, fighting for their beliefs and spilling blood to prove their worth. After all of their wounds, after the paring down of their humanity and their lives to nothing but shell-shocked nubs, she could give them respite.

She inhaled deeply, raising her arms and spreading them wide.

Famine called out, "What are you doing?"

Without looking back, Missy replied, "Getting my Sword."

She opened herself to the red tide of power that was War. It careened through her, a torrent of energy that sizzled through her blood, drowning her and burning her, consuming her and renewing her until she was a phoenix arising from her own ashes. With a rapturous cry, she summoned the Sword to her. It appeared in her hand, the perfect blade, a thing of crystalline murder.

Melissa Miller, avatar of War, bellowed her challenge to the world. Wrapped in a red haze, she sliced through the refugees and the warriors and the humanitarians and the civilians caught in the warzone—everyone within a twenty-mile radius. The Sword cut deeply, carving into emotions and sawing through states of mind.

War wielded her blade, and around her, people bled.

She felt them all, from the wizened refugee whose bare feet had been misshapen by the desert rocks, to the young fighter in the village beyond the mountains who'd vomited as he made his first kill this very day, to the child living with her family under the bridge because the gunfire was too strong for them to make a run to the relative safety of the school building— Missy felt them and more than a quarter million others. These were her people—defined by war, shaped by blood, tempered by need. She screeched with their pain, with their fear and on-going terror; she ached with their constant sorrow and pulsing bitterness that ate at their souls; she groaned from their con-stant exhaustion of not knowing if today was the day there

would be no food, no shelter, no sanctuary. Missy felt everything as her people bled out their badness. She took it away
from them, snatched it like a thief.

And then, catharsis.

Purged of their overwhelming burdens, at least for the moment, her people breathed easily. Children ran with renewed
energy. Babies nestled in their mothers' arms, lulled with the
sleepy satisfaction of being loved. Adults smiled, contented by
the sounds and sights of the children at play. And beyond the
mountains, the war halted as soldiers on both sides felt no urge
to fight.

In the sea of refugees, Melissa Miller sank to the ground, exhausted. The red wave receded, leaving her limbs trembling and
her heart pounding and a stitch in her side that felt as if she'd
been gutted with a spear. She closed her eyes, and War heard the
negotiations begin anew, to get the supply trucks first through to
those civilians enmeshed in the battle-scarred town and then beyond, to those who had taken their children and fled.

As bone-weary as Missy was, she grinned. She had helped.
It wasn't much, and it wasn't permanent. But it was a start. It
was a spark of hope, here in this place where hope had been as
rare as desert snow.

"It does snow here, occasionally," Famine said. "The locals
never know what to make of it."

Missy opened her eyes to see Famine offering her a hand.

"The trucks will go through," Famine said. "The people
here may still starve. And they may still slaughter one another
in the name of justice. But not today." Her grin cut through
the shadow of her face. "This is more like it for your first day
on the job."

Missy blinked stupidly at the black-gloved hand. And then she accepted it, and Famine pulled War to her feet.

"Never could stand it when people sulked," the Black Rider said.

|||||

Missy had to make a pit stop before she went home. The girls' locker room reeked with the acrid smell of ammonia. At least no one had defecated in her bag. That had to count for something, right?

Ares allowed her to load the duffle bag on to the saddle, although the horse snorted sharply.

"I know," Missy said. "It sucks. People suck sometimes." Life sucked sometimes, and that was the truth of it. The thought made her think of Adam, of his easy lie about how he'd missed her. Strangely, that stung even worse than how he'd played her so completely. *Let me make it up to you,* he'd said, and she'd been so ready to believe him.

She had been such a fool.

The warhorse blew out a question punctuated by a flicking of its ears.

Missy didn't need to speak Horse to understand. She smiled faintly as she scratched behind its ears. "I'm okay," she lied. "Just tired." Yes, that too. She pulled herself onto the saddle and asked Ares to take her home.

After taking her to her front door, Ares whinnied a farewell before leaping into the sky. She watched the steed until it was out of sight, and then she fished out her house key from her wet bag. At least she'd had it in the side compartment, away from the worst of the soaking clothes. It struck her as grossly unfair that after she had helped hundreds of thousands of people today, she was left holding a bag of urine-soaked clothing.

Life *really* sucked sometimes.

The house greeted her with silence. It was similar to the quiet that came after a session with her razor: empty, peaceful, the stillness of a leaf after a slow-motion tumble to the grassy floor. There was no need for her to check the calendar posted on the refrigerator; she knew the schedule by heart—her mom and sister were off at their mother-daughter book club before Sue had Cheer and her mom had an afternoon out with friends; her dad was at the office until God knew when. Missy was alone.

Missy had been alone a long, long time. An empty house was nothing more than a physical reminder.

The enormity of the day's events crashed down on her as she marched downstairs to the laundry room, where she dropped her soiled duffle bag and stripped off her gloves. She had traveled to a distant land, on horseback, all in the blink of an eye. The wind had whipped her hair hard enough to sting her face, and the desert sun had been merciless.

Missy unlaced her cleats and peeled off her socks.

She'd heard the firecracker pops of gunfire, had smelled the unwashed bodies of a quarter million people spread over the dusty ground like rancid human butter.

Missy unstrapped her shin guards and shucked off her shorts.

She had felt their pain, and with Famine beside her she had eaten their fear. A taste lingered in her mouth, like bittersweet chocolate.

Missy pulled off her goalie shirt.

She had cut them open and revealed their tortured hearts. She had bled them out and left them with the hope of salvation.

Missy threw her dirty laundry, bag and all, into the washing machine and added detergent.

She thought of a little boy, or maybe a girl, laughing in delight and kicking a ball with dirty bare feet over the hot, rocky ground of the desert, oblivious to the misery that weighted down the air. The toddler chased the ball, and on the other side of the mountains, delivery trucks began their long-delayed runs.

Missy started the wash cycle, tossed her soccer equipment onto the mat in the corner, then trudged up the stairs, clad only in her sports bra and underwear.

And before all that, Missy's team had won the game.

She had done all that—her, Melissa Miller. *She* had done that.

War can be a tragedy, certainly. But you could be something more.

For today, she had been that something more. Grinning, she fell onto her bed, her sweat and scars mingling as she lay prone, too tired to do more than just breathe.

Her life waited for her: the aftermath of the party loomed, and Monday was fast approaching. But that would wait. Later, she'd begin picking up the pieces of her life. She thought of Famine, remembered her cautionary tale of Pestilence. Missy couldn't undo what had been done. But maybe, like the White Rider, she could rein in the damage. At the very least, she could prevent it from getting worse.

And hopefully, it wouldn't take her five hundred years to fix.

Later, she told herself again. She'd figure it out later. For now, it was just her on her bed, safe in her room—no desert winds, no supernatural threats, no urges to pick up her razor and split her skin. For now, it was just the memory of winning the game, and the ghost of her cat nuzzling in her usual spot, settling in the crook of Missy's elbow.

For now, it was good.

As she drifted off, she felt a blanket cover her, then a kiss of frost against her brow. She would have smiled, but she was already fast asleep.

CHAPTER 12

The phone woke Missy two hours later. With a groan, she buried her head under her pillow, but the answering machine volume had been set to Obnoxiously High, so even up in her bedroom Missy could hear the muffled sounds of a girl leaving a message. She closed her eyes and tried to will herself back to sleep, but no luck—she was up.

Sighing, she sat up in bed. And then she blinked as she saw she was all but naked. What had she been thinking, crashing out without a long-sleeved nightshirt? All she needed was for her mom to duck her head in at the wrong time and see Missy's scars. That would have been the end of everything.

She has to go home and cry to her mommy.

No. No, no, no. She didn't want to think about Adam, about the shreds of her social life. Not now. Not ever.

Missy grabbed clothing from her bureau, intending to just throw on any old outfit, but as she looked at the black and black and black, she thought of a painfully thin woman shrouded in shadow. So Missy rummaged, and she pulled out a bright red long-sleeved shirt adorned with a vampire's smile, along with red stockings and tattered black shorts that had faded to a soft gray. There. She was practically dripping with cheer.

That made her think of her sister in her Cheer uniform, a plastic smile on her face as she told Missy that she was a sick excuse of a sister.

No. *No.*

To make sure she wasn't thinking about Adam or Sue or her life in general, Missy stormed down to the laundry room to throw the stuff currently in the washer into the dryer. She was too keyed up to eat, so she retreated to her room to attack her homework.

Three hours later, Missy was studying for Monday's pre-calculus test. Her peed-on clothing and soccer uniform were clean once more and already folded neatly in their drawers; her duffle bag was on the mat in the laundry room, along with her now clean soccer equipment. It had taken her a while to get all the grass and dirt out of her cleats, and the process had ruined her nails. But damn if it hadn't felt good.

She had finished her homework and had one more chapter to review—forget idle threats by Famine, logarithms were going to be the death of her—and then it would be on to frozen pizza and a movie. She already had a flick picked out, an oldie but goodie that she and Erica used to love to watch. A boy gives a girl his heart, and she gives him a pen. The pen, in this case, was mightier than the sword.

WHETHER FROM A PLAYWRIGHT OR A PROPHET, War said, IT'S NOTHING BUT WORDS.

Maybe so. But words mattered.

Freak, Adam whispered.

Some words clearly mattered more than others. She shoved thoughts of Adam away and threw herself into math as if she were smothering a grenade.

Missy was reviewing the relationship between distance, speed, and time (and wondering idly about the metaphysics of traveling half the world by flying steed and returning to find less than an hour had passed) when the house phone rang. Once again, the machine picked up; once again, a girl's muffled voice left Charlie Brown grownup sounds, all whines and meaningless tones. Missy thumbed the tip of her pen, felt the indent press against the sensitive pad of her finger as the caller rambled.

Finally, silence.

It was probably Sue, leaving Mom and Dad a message. Sue always did the right thing, at least to their parents' faces. She always called. She always smiled when they were looking, always was a team player. Sue was the perfect daughter; Missy saw that reflected in their parents' eyes every time they looked at her. Sue didn't wear clothing that made her look like a starving artist; Sue didn't put on enough makeup to give hookers a run for their money. Their parents never complained about Missy's chosen appearance. They didn't have to; they had Sue.

Missy padded her way downstairs to listen to her perfect sister's perfect message. A big red number two greeted her, reminding her of the call that had woken her from her nap. She pressed Play on the answering machine and grabbed a glass from the drying rack.

"Hey, Missy. It's Erica."

Missy froze, glass in hand.

"Call me, okay?" That was the first message. Erica's second, and last, message, was more imploring:

"I've texted and emailed, and I even left you voice mail on your cell, but maybe you're offline. Don't blame you for that. I just, you know, want to make sure you're okay. Last night was really harsh."

Missy's breath was coming too fast; her blood was pounding behind her eyes, roaring in her ears.

"So, um, give me a call, okay? Or text me. Just, you know, let me know that you're okay. Okay? Thanks. Bye."

Missy hit Erase so hard that she broke her nail. She slammed the glass on the counter.

What the hell had Erica been thinking? Her parents could have heard that. Missy would have been bombarded by questions, by accusations. They never would have left her alone, not until she admitted what Adam had done to her.

Sue's voice, hissing in rage and bitter disappointment: *I'm embarrassed to know you.*

Missy clamped her hands over her forearms and hugged herself, shivering. She wanted to cut and cut and cut, wanted to saw away at her flesh until her blood made it all better. She wanted the razor to caress her, its kisses stinging her like frostbite. And if she cut too much, or too deeply, well, would that be so bad?

I don't need the blade, she thought desperately. *I don't. I don't. I don't.*

Death's fingers along her cheek, colder than ice; his voice, heating her body with just one word: *control.*

Maybe it wasn't as awful as she feared. Maybe Adam and the others got a good laugh at her expense, and that was the end of it.

Maybe.

Maybe.

Hope in five small letters. She clung onto the idea of *maybe,* but it wasn't quite enough to pull her from the undertow of despair.

She had to know. She had to go online, right now, had to check her messages and see for herself that Adam hadn't done anything worse than shred her dignity and pocket some cash. She dashed out of the kitchen. She'd prove to herself that her life wasn't over, and then she'd eat and do her studying and figure out how to rebuild what Adam had demolished.

In her room, she picked up her cell phone and turned it on for the first time since Friday evening. She had twenty-seven text messages waiting, and three videos in queue.

Oh, God.

She had one voice mail message and five missed calls. All the missed calls were from Erica.

Okay. She blew out a breath and tackled the voice mail first. Voice mail was easy. Voice mail was one-to-one, simple to review and erase and move on. It was also from Erica, asking if Missy was all right.

Was she? She didn't know, not yet. Swallowing thickly, she keyed up her text messages.

The first one simply said HAHAHA!!!!! She didn't recognize the sender's number. Delete.

The second one called her a CUTTERSLUT. Three guesses who that was from. Delete.

The third was from Jenna, and it said that Missy was gross and emo and pathetic. Yeah, well, minus the emo, that also described Jenna, so there you go. Delete.

The fourth was from Trudy, and all it said was LOOSER. Missy hit Reply and texted back: Spell your insults properly, LOSER. Smiling grimly, Missy hit Send and then deleted Trudy's message.

Okay. Twenty-three to go. And if even one more was from Trudy, not only could Missy handle it, she would even bust a gut laughing. Encouraged, she checked the fifth message.

NEXT TIME SLICE UR WRISTS THE LONG WAY 2 GET IT RITE

She didn't recognize the sender's number. Or maybe that was from the sudden blur of tears. Delete delete delete.

The next ten messages were more of the same. All from different numbers. All of them telling her to just kill herself already. She couldn't bear to read the others. Erica's was probably in there somewhere, but she couldn't wade through the hatred to find that one small breath of compassion.

That left the video messages. She didn't want to look.

She had to look.

Shaking, she saw the first video. She was on the bed in Kevin's room, startled by all of the voyeurs, stunned by Adam's betrayal. Her scars looked particularly livid on the small screen. Her mouth was working, but Missy couldn't hear herself over the sound of raucous laughter. She deleted that video, as well as the two others—no need to watch those. Then she dropped her phone to the floor, crawled to her garbage can, and vomited.

It wasn't as bad as she'd feared.

It was worse. Oh, God, it was so much worse.

She wiped her mouth and stared dully at her closet. On her door, Marilyn Monroe smiled, oblivious, eyes shut against the harshness of the world. James Dean simply looked away.

Inside the closet, her lockbox waited.

Inside the closet was her one true friend.

Inside the closet was the only way to make everything right. A whisper of steel, a moment of pain, and then everything would be right.

I don't need the blade. I don't need the blade. I don't.

She did.

Staring at her closet door, she picked up her cell phone. She dialed a number she'd thought she'd forgotten, because it had been months since Missy had been anything close to a real friend. Erica picked up on the second ring.

"I want to die," Missy said, her soul naked and raw.

"I'll be there in two minutes," Erica said.

||||||

"This is my favorite part," Erica said.

The girls watched as, onscreen, Lloyd Dobbler held up a huge portable radio—a boom box, according to Missy's parents—so that Diane Court could better hear the song playing. Diane tossed and turned in her bed as the singer passionately spoke of what he saw in her eyes. Cut to Lloyd, his own eyes full of hope, spelled M-A-Y-B-E.

Hope was nothing more than a joke.

Erica sighed happily. "It's the most romantic thing I've ever seen, you know?"

Missy did. It was one of the reasons she loved this movie. There had been a time when she'd thought Adam had been her Lloyd, the boy who would strive to understand her and make her laugh and simply want to be with her, even with her imperfections. "It's fiction," Missy said. "Of course it's romantic."

She felt Erica's stare, but Missy didn't pull her gaze away from the television. Erica had come over, taken one look at Missy, and hugged her until Missy's ribs ached. She'd tried to get Missy to talk, but that was the last thing Missy wanted to do. Talking was pointless; Erica wouldn't understand, even if

Missy had been able to wrap up all her feelings into words and could string them together into a coherent sentence. So Erica said, "Let's watch a movie." Missy pulled out *Say Anything;* Erica put a bag of popcorn in the microwave. Five minutes later, the girls were on the sofa in the family room, watching Lloyd and Diane slowly fall in love.

"Romance happens in real life," Erica said.

"Only the air-quotes kind of romance."

"That's not true. My parents are still stupidly in love," Erica insisted. "They look at each other when they think no one's watching and make googly eyes, and they kiss all the time, and they have these lame jokes that they always laugh at." She smiled a goofy, hopeful smile. "And if it happened for them, it can happen for me. For you too."

Missy thought that was a crock, but she said nothing.

They watched the rest of the movie, complete with its storybook ending: love triumphed over all. For now. Roll credits. Neither girl moved to take out the DVD.

"I miss this," Erica said. "You know, just hanging. Watching movies. Talking," she added, throwing in a look heavy with meaning.

Missy picked up one of the small pillows that were everywhere on the sofa, and she hugged it to her chest. "Talking about what?"

The other girl started to say something, then closed her mouth. She fumbled with the tassels on another pillow before she admitted, "I don't want you getting mad at me."

The words slapped Missy. This girl had been her best friend once upon a time, both of them princesses in the Land of

Stuffed Animals and Barbie Dolls. When had Missy stopped hanging out with her? Well before Adam, before soccer. Middle school, she realized. Eighth grade: just as the balance between school and family and social life, always difficult, had suddenly become precarious. Had she walked away from Erica because of the ongoing pressure to not simply achieve but to excel—because of expectations, carefully wrapped in parental encouragement and delivered in pipe bomb packages of hormones? That was the time Missy had discovered her new best friend, her true love with kisses that left her bleeding and peaceful, if only for a little while. Missy had traded Erica for her razor, and she hadn't looked back.

Truth be told, she hadn't noticed. She had woken up one day with a secret written on her arms and no one to share it with.

"I won't get mad at you," Missy said thickly.

Erica said, "I knew before yesterday about, you know. You cutting. Some people just assume it because you're goth, but I saw, once, on your left wrist. Your sleeve had gotten bunched up, and there were all these lines, these raised pink lines, and I thought to myself, *Missy's cutting.*"

"I'm not goth," Missy said, but her words were lost in the sudden booming of her heartbeat. Erica knew. Erica had known. Erica hadn't said anything. That echoed in her head, keeping time to the pounding of her heart.

"Goth, emo. Whatever. I don't know what the difference is, anyway." Erica fumbled with her pillow. "What's it like? When you cut, I mean. What's it feel like?"

At first, Missy couldn't reply; she was swimming in the Red, her heart tattooing a beat with every stroke.

SHE'LL BETRAY YOU, War whispered. *THAT'S ALL PEOPLE DO. THEY USE YOU AND BETRAY YOU. THEY EAT YOUR TRUST AND SPIT OUT YOUR HEART.*

Erica wouldn't.

And even if Erica would, Missy thought, what was there to hide? How could Erica hurt her any worse than she had already been hurt?

What if Erica was sincere? What if she wanted to help?

Missy hugged her pillow tightly. So many what-ifs. So many chances for hope, all ready to be dashed to bits upon the floor.

Missy took a deep breath, then let it out in a shaky exhale. "It hurts," she said. "If I do it right, and I go slow and shallow, it really hurts. Like getting stung by wasps, or pulling off a hangnail that's the size of your thumb, and all of it is happening in slow motion."

Something close to horror shone in Erica's eyes, even though the rest of her face was calm. "So you're into getting hurt?"

"No," Missy said. "It's not about enjoying pain. I'm not like, you know, a masochist or anything."

Erica frowned. "So why do you cut?"

She's trying, Missy thought. Erica was trying to understand. Missy fumbled, searching for the right words. "When I cut, I'm the one controlling the pain. I know where it's coming from. I know that it's me who's doing it, me and no one else." God, she felt stupid. She wasn't explaining it right. She sounded like an idiot. "It's better than the other pain."

Freak, Adam whispered, almost lovingly.

Erica asked, "What other pain?"

"The one in my chest," Missy said softly, but gripping the

pillow tight tight tight. "The one that crushes everything else. The one that makes it impossible to breathe."

Erica picked up a tassel-covered pillow and held it and said nothing. Missy, numb with fear, watched the television screen, frozen on the movie menu. Erica was going to call her a freak. Erica was going to laugh at her, going to walk away and leave Missy alone with the Sword in her head and blood on her hands.

"Cutting is messed up," Erica finally said, plucking at the tassels on her pillow. "But I get why you do it. At home, I cry in my pillow. You cut yourself. I get it. I understand feeling like you're going to die." She paused. "But when I cry, I'm not hurting myself. I'm letting it out."

"Cutting lets it out."

"Yeah, but crying doesn't make you bleed." She turned to look at Missy. "You should talk to someone. You know, not just me. Someone to help you stop cutting."

Missy thought of a man who wasn't a man, heard his laughter, felt his cold touch dance over her skin. "You're right," she agreed. "Someone's trying to help me."

Erica blinked, then smiled, and the movement transformed her from a mousy girl into a beautiful young woman. It was the smile of an angel being thanked with a child's joyful laugh. "Good. You should let them."

"I'm trying."

"Good," Erica said again.

Missy understood that Erica thought Missy was talking about Erica herself. Missy had been a lousy friend lately, but she wasn't so far gone that she'd tell Erica the truth. Besides, especially with the goth and emo comments, Missy didn't think that Erica would understand if Missy admitted that she was crushing on Death. So she just smiled back and thought about the Pale Rider with his haunting eyes and winter-touched voice, and she suggested they watch another movie.

About two hours later, Erica headed back home, making Missy swear to call if she started feeling lousy.

"Don't cut," Erica said as she left.

"I won't," Missy promised, then shut the door behind her.

"Cut what?"

Missy jumped at the sound of her father's voice. He must have come in through the garage door. She turned to see him taking off his jacket and looking at her oddly.

I could tell him, she thought wildly. *Tell him just like I told Erica. I could tell him, and maybe he and Mom would get it.*

Or maybe they would send her away to a white room with padded walls.

"Junior skip day's Monday," she lied smoothly. "Most of the class is cutting. But I've got a pre-calc test, so I won't."

"To say nothing of how cutting classes is wrong," said her father.

"Very wrong," Missy agreed.

Her father laughed softly as he hung his jacket in the hall closet. "It hasn't been that long since I was in high school. I'd been known to cut here and there."

Missy thought of her razor and smiled ruefully. "I'm sure."

SUNDAY

CHAPTER 13

In her dream, Melissa Miller is inside a volcano, having tea with War. Missy doesn't care for tea, but it's what civilized people do, and so she pours hot water into War's porcelain cup and offers the sugar jar. War declines.

Sitting on a throne of molten rock, the Red Rider looms, a massive being in silver armor overlaying crimson mesh. The image of a blood-red sword adorns War's breastplate. Large gauntlets cover powerful hands; enormous boots encase feet and legs meant to kick down barricades. A silver helm covers War's head; the faceguard is elaborate and foreboding to gaze upon, and it completely obscures War's face. A fiery plume at the top of the helm flutters playfully, its feathers ruffling in the volcano's updraft.

Missy sits opposite War. She, too, is dressed for battle: her long-sleeved goalie shirt fits snugly, and her cleats sink into the volcanic rock. Holding the teacup is difficult with her soccer gloves, but she manages.

"HAVE YOU DECIDED?" War asks, lifting the tiny cup.

Missy mirrors the gesture. "No."

"IT WILL GO BETTER FOR YOU IF YOU DO IT OF YOUR OWN ACCORD. I CAN BE PATIENT, AS EVEN DEATH WOULD ATTEST. BUT EVENTUALLY, PATIENCE WEARS THIN." War's voice echoes in the volcano, and far below, the magma ripples.

"You want me to embrace you," says Missy, frowning over her teacup. "I don't see how that would help me."

"I CARE NOTHING FOR HELPING YOU. THIS IS NOT ABOUT YOU AT ALL. I CARE ONLY TO RIDE."

"I must make a thoughtful decision. Pestilence didn't think ahead," says Missy, "and look what happened."

"THIS ISN'T ABOUT THE WHITE RIDER. AND YOU PUT TOO MUCH STOCK IN THE WORDS OF ANOTHER HORSEMAN. NONE OF THE OTHERS UNDERSTANDS WHAT IT MEANS TO BE IN THE THROES OF PASSION." *Within the helm, War's eyes glitter like rubies.* "YOU AND I, WE UNDERSTAND THE NEED FOR STEEL, THE URGE FOR BLOOD. WE SEEK OUR PLEASURE FROM PAIN."

"This is not civilized conversation. Drink your tea," says Missy.

War sets down the cup. Liquid sloshes over the sides and evaporates in the heat of the volcano. "THE TEA IS WEAK."

(freak)

"YOU ARE WEAK."

(freak)

"You don't know me," Missy whispers, clutching her teacup tightly. "You know nothing of me."

"I KNOW YOU ARE STRONG ENOUGH TO DRIVE PEOPLE TO THEIR KNEES," *says War,* "AND YET YOU SWALLOW YOUR RAGE AND COUCH IT IN TERMS OF BOYFRIENDS AND SISTERS. YOU DEFLECT WHEN YOU SHOULD STRIKE. YOU ARE WEAK."

(freak you're nothing but a freak)

Below them, the magma begins to rise.

War, too, rises, offering a gauntleted hand to Missy. "YOU CAN BE SO MUCH MORE. EMBRACE ME, AND I WILL TAKE YOU TO PLACES YOU CANNOT BEGIN TO IMAGINE."

"I have not yet decided," Missy insists, watching the orange-red floor yawn its way closer. She feels oddly content. She is Death's Handmaiden; the notion of dying holds no fear to her.

But War doesn't want her to die. War wants her to live. And that is ever so much harder.

"EMBRACE ME," *says War,* "AND I WILL GIVE YOU THE WORLD."

"I have not yet decided." Missy sips her tea, but it has gone cold.

"EMBRACE ME," *War bellows,* "OR I WILL TAKE WHAT I WANT!"

The magma roils, and it reaches for them with fingers hotter than passion. The sword gleams on War's breastplate as the fire takes them.

▌▌▌▌▌

She awoke suddenly, caught in that state between dreaming and fully conscious, and for a long moment she didn't know who she was. A metallic taste lingered in her mouth— spilled blood, spiced with emotion. Her blood; she had bitten her lip in her sleep. As for the emotion, she couldn't put a name to it.

FEAR. THAT'S FEAR YOU'RE FEELING. IT'S QUICKENING YOUR HEART AND TRIPPING YOUR BREATH. IT'S POPPING SWEAT ON YOUR BROW. YOU'RE AFRAID.

Cold words; heated intention. The voice was a thing of frozen fire, chilling her and singeing her until she was nothing more than a cinder buried in snow.

YOU'RE AFRAID OF ME.

No, she thought. *Not of you. I'm afraid of* me. *Who am I?* Shivering, she wrapped the blanket around her and swallowed blood. *What am I?*

A FLAWED SKIN. A DEFECTIVE SHELL.

No, she was more than that. She had to be. She was . . .

A VESSEL, AND DAMAGED AT THAT. THAT IS ALL YOU ARE.

A notion of *being* dangled before her, then danced away in a pirouetting of noontime shadow. Back again: a glint of identity, bright as sunlight on metal. Yes, she had it. She was—

"Missy," she said aloud, her voice breaking. "I'm Missy."

Oh, thank God. She had a name.

She closed her eyes and breathed, then breathed some more. She knew who she was: Melissa Miller, sixteen, self-injurer. Beneath her thick comforter, she rubbed her arms, feeling the raised flesh of her scars as she traced their lines. "Scars," she whispered. The word itself was like a cut: the initial smooth motion of the *S* as she raises the blade; the quick flash of the hard *C*, biting her skin; the fluid *AR* as her blood wells; the final, lazy *S*, leaking out of her, mixed with all the badness that had made breathing so very difficult.

"Scars," she said again, firmer. Instant gratification forever branded on her flesh. When she would cut, she wouldn't think about things like consequence; all that mattered was forcing the Too Much to bend into something manageable, bearable. She ran her thumb along the crook of her elbow, secret rendezvous of too many razor kisses to count. After cutting, it was all about hiding her actions, as if she'd committed a crime.

Laughter in her mind, like the sound of steel ringing against steel.

A crime? Ridiculous. What she chose to do to herself wasn't anyone's choice but her own. She nodded to herself as her thumbnail pressed against her elbow crease, moving back and forth, back and forth. The only one she was hurting was herself; it wasn't as if she were a sociopath in training.

. . . Graygirl, limp in her arms, her final warbling meow already fading . . .

Frowning, Missy shoved the memory away. This wasn't about what she'd done to her cat two months ago. This wasn't about anyone, anything, other than Missy herself.

Steel chimed; a blade sliced through the air, making music in the wind.

She opened her eyes, blind to the anger simmering in her gaze. Yes, she cut herself sometimes. She did what she needed to do, and if people didn't understand that, that was their problem, not hers.

Her lip curled into a sneer. *Their* problem. *They* always had a problem, didn't they? Whether it was with her clothing or her attitude, her grades or her scars. *They* would always find fault with her.

And she let them.

Not my problem, she screamed silently, directing her fury to the heavens as tears scorched tracks down her cheeks. *I don't have a problem. I don't!*

Tucked away in its lockbox, her razor beckoned.

It would be so easy to take it out, to touch the blade to her thigh and let it taste the salt of her skin, the penny-sweet tang of her blood. She scraped her thumbnail against the curve of her elbow, biting deep. But it wasn't the same.

Don't cut, Erica whispered.

Missy scrubbed away her tears and told her friend to shut up. Her thumbnail, ragged and wet along its edge, rubbed against her cheek. Blood and salt water mixed on her face, pale fluid mingling with red.

Erica's voice again, a whisper, maybe a plea: *Crying doesn't make you bleed.*

Missy blotted the wetness with her shirtsleeve. Enough. She wasn't about to argue with a memory, not at—she glanced at the alarm clock on her nightstand—3:13 in the morning. *Three o'clock, and all's well.*

Yeah, right.

Missy took a deep breath and let it out slowly. So she'd had a bad dream and had woken up disoriented. That happened, even to normal people who didn't have Swords and warhorses and a slight crush on Death. A bad dream, and nothing more.

So never mind the lingering notion that she didn't know who she was. That was just a dark corner in her brain, detritus in the soup pot of her mind. Everything would settle back into place and she'd go back to knowing exactly what she was: an outcast, a lone ship with no safe harbor, forced to sail through the shark-infested seas of high school.

Oh, God. How was she going to make it through Monday? Everyone would know by then what Adam had done to her. How was she supposed to walk down the halls? Sit in class? Act normal? She swallowed thickly.

Fear, War murmured.

No, stop. Monday wasn't for another twenty-some-odd hours. She didn't need to freak about it now. She needed to go back to sleep. That's what normal people did, right? She told her heartbeat to slow down. It ignored her. And now the rest of her body was following suit—she started feeling *up,* that *gotta-move* feeling she got before a soccer game. Fight or flight, baby. Monday was coming.

Fight or flight.

She sat up, clutching the blanket to her chest.

Come out and grab the ball, Bella taunted, her voice playful rather than cruel. *I dare you.*

Missy got out of bed and went to her window. Outside, dappled by moonlight, Ares waited for her. She wished it had surprised her, but part of her had known her steed would be there.

Now? she thought, staring at the red horse. She was supposed to go out now, in the middle of the night, and play War?

The warhorse snorted as if in agreement. Or maybe it was just chiding her to hurry up already; the night wasn't waiting for her.

Waiting for me, Missy thought, turning away from the window. *But which me?* Did the steed follow the girl with the penchant for razors and withering gazes? Or was it the Red Rider that Ares waited upon? Which face did the red steed see when it looked at her?

Who am I? she wondered as she pulled on a pair of jeans.

If Ares had an answer, the steed kept it to itself.

||||||

They flew, War on her steed, the two of them ripping a path across the dark sky.

Her hair whipping her face, her heartbeat surging in her ears, Missy gripped the reins and dug in her heels. Escaping her life, even for a stolen moment in a witching-hour ride, felt deliriously good. Up here, with only the stars and moon to bear witness, she didn't have to think of the dread reality that waited for her by sunlight. Up here, she could lose herself without consequence, without needing to reach for the razor or strap on her dead face. There was freedom to be found among the stars. Maybe she wasn't sure who she was. But in the sky, on her steed, it didn't matter. She *was*. That was enough.

Beneath them, people dreamed, their emotions colored in bleeding reds and harsh blacks, in furious greens and slick yellows. Missy felt them all, experienced those small wars and savored the sensations. Soon she was feeding on those feelings, sipping joy and nibbling despair. Feasting on desire. Gorging on anger. Drunk with emotion, she flew onward. And below, people's dreams turned violent. Some muttered dark things as they slept, things that would stay with them once they woke. In the morning, they would glare at loved ones and find all manner of things unspeakably foul. Their days were ruined long before they even opened their eyes.

Melissa Miller's mouth stretched into a wide grin, but it was War who rumbled laughter.

Soon, though, reds and blacks gave way to white, and the feeling of sickness slithered along Missy's limbs, coating her in rancid butter. She slapped at it, but it dug deep, getting under her skin. Suddenly lightheaded, Missy leaned down to clasp Ares' neck.

Sick. She was sick.

No. Something was *making* her sick.

She frowned down at the town sleeping below. There. The feeling was centered somewhere down there. She debated whether to fly on and ride past that sickly feeling of white, but something about it had hooked her curiosity. What was the harm in looking? She had her Sword. She had Ares. Nothing could hurt her; she had already been hurt far too much to fear small things like minor dizziness. She nudged Ares and told him to land.

The horse snorted, clearly displeased, but it did as it was told. It was a good steed.

YOU'RE A FOOL TO THINK SUCH THINGS, said War. THE BEAST WOULD KILL YOU AS SOON AS LOOK AT YOU.

Missy remembered how Ares had come to her defense when she had first met Famine.

GIVEN THE CHANCE, YOUR STEED WOULD BETRAY YOU, AS QUICK AS A STAB TO THE HEART. IT'S A WARHORSE. IT KNOWS NOTHING OF COMPASSION. IT CARES NOTHING FOR PRAISE.

They landed before Missy knew how to respond, which was probably for the best.

Ares' hooves touched down in a gallop, and as the warhorse slowed, Missy took in their surroundings. By day, the shopping mall could have been home to a thousand stores, with a million customers tearing through the bargain racks. But now it was just a stage prop: a massive chain of buildings, brooding and dark. The parking lot sprawled, empty, its neat rows of spots grinning. Refuse dotted the lot in clumps, blackheads on the face of the asphalt. It smelled of hollow soda cans and dead cigarettes.

Deeper than the smells, though, was the sensation of illness that she had felt in the air; it was a greasy white coating that clogged Missy's pores. She sneezed once, violently. Wiping her nose on her sleeve, she blinked, then blinked again.

Faint white lines pulsed on the blacktop, threading through the lot and leading out of the shopping mall. Missy was certain those lines hadn't been there a moment ago. Looking at them made her head spin; looking away from them wrenched her heart.

She thought of every horror movie she had ever seen, and she knew that following that glowing trail was a Very Bad Idea.

But she also knew she *had* to follow it; something about that white path called to her even as it turned her stomach.

Well, she thought, *if I die, I get to see Death again.*

Picturing Death dressed in a dead musician's skin, Missy urged Ares to follow the faint white threads out of the empty lot. A steady *clop-clop-clop* of hooves on pavement hung in the still air, the background noise of a disembodied heartbeat. The main road stretched away from the mall in a sharp curve, framed on either side by the thick woods of undeveloped land. Deer country, based on the big warning sign to drivers: watch out for jumping deer. If not for the mostly full moon, Missy would have been all but blind. Apparently, roads populated by jumping deer didn't have streetlights.

As they walked, that sense of sickness, of *wrongness,* grew stronger. Mere lightheadedness became severe dizziness, and her stomach pitched and rolled. Missy darted glances to either side, unnerved by the enormous trees. They stood in the dark, impassive, silently observing the road. Unseen leaves rustled in the wind, the sound like soft laughter. Missy felt their wooden eyes on her, watching her, waiting to see if she would be tempted like Little Red Riding Hood and traipse off the path. Waiting to see if they could show her their teeth.

Always follow the ball, Bella warned. *Don't look away too long.*

Missy snapped her gaze back to the faintly glowing trail, ignoring the black trees that stood sentry. Though the nighttime air had a bite to it, she began to sweat. *This is crazy,* she told herself. *Alone at three in the morning, out in the night.* She should go home, go to bed.

Go home, Adam sneered, *and cry to your mommy.*

Missy swallowed thickly and nudged Ares to keep going.

About a mile down the road, the path came to an abrupt end at the feet of a man in white, his clothing so bright, it seemed to glow. The man sat in the dirt, his back against a tree, his gloved fingers laced together as he slowly rocked. A white horse, its coat as bright as the man's, stood near him.

Missy coaxed Ares to a halt. Though she hadn't known exactly what to expect, it hadn't been this. But considering how her life had been going the past day or so, she shouldn't have been surprised. Staring at the man, trying to ignore the way she felt like she was going to vomit any second, she slid off her steed. She landed with her knees bent and feet wide, ready to move, to run, to launch herself into the air to block the goal. But there was no soccer ball coming her way; no opposing team player charged her. There was only the man, in his pristinely white coat and pants, rocking in the dirt, muttering.

She opened her mouth to ask if he was all right, but she inhaled poison. Choking, Missy doubled over. This wasn't drowning in overwhelming emotions, suffocating by wants and needs and desires—she couldn't breathe because the air itself was heavy with disease. Panicking, she tried to stop coughing, and that made her cough all the harder.

Control.

She didn't know if that was her thought or War's or Death's, and it didn't matter. Gagging, she drew the Sword and sliced through the toxic air, parting it in a shower of sparks. Clean air rushed through the rip, flooding over her. She gulped in a breath, and then another. Her throat screamed for water, and her chest burned. But she could breathe again.

Missy stood tall, her nausea momentarily subdued, the Sword naked in her hand. Her eyes narrowed as she glared at the white-clad man.

HE ATTACKED YOU, War whispered.

Around the hilt, her knuckles whitened. How *dare* he attack her? She had come to help.

HE BETRAYED YOU. THEY ALL BETRAY YOU. CUT HIM DOWN.

Her arm trembled with the need to raise the Sword high and slash it across the man's chest.

FEEL HOW WARM HIS BLOOD IS. CUT HIM DOWN.

His white coat would make his blood brilliantly scarlet, like a cardinal in snow. It would be beautiful. Magnificent.

CUT HIM DOWN!

She gripped the hilt in both hands now. The edges of her vision were tinged with red, and her blood roared in her ears. She could kill him. She should kill him. It would be so easy. She lifted the Sword . . . and then she heard it again: that quiet voice, his voice, cautioning her and encouraging her.

Control.

Missy took a deep breath, and she slowly lowered the Sword.

If the man noticed her, or recognized how close he'd come to meeting the business end of her blade, he didn't show it. He continued rocking, and mumbling, and dry-washing his gloved hands. His head hung low; long black hair shrouded his face.

Her anger fizzled and died. She couldn't be mad, not when there was clearly something wrong with him. He didn't try to attack her—he was sick. She sheathed her Sword and took a step forward.

Ares snorted, pawing the ground.

"Stay there," she ordered, not looking back. She sensed the warhorse settling down, felt its tension radiating in nuclear fury. It didn't like her approaching the man in white, not without the Sword raised for battle, but it would do as she commanded. She knew that, just as she knew her name was Melissa Miller.

She took another step toward the man. Now she was close enough to see something glinting in his hair, catching the moonlight and winking silver. The white horse blinked at her, but it didn't move to stop her.

"Excuse me," she called out. "Are you all right?"

The man whipped his head up. On his brow, a silver crown gleamed in startling contrast to his black hair. His face was a thing of horrors—waxy and riddled with growths, his mouth swimming in cold sores. "'All right,' 'all right.' Always they want to know if you're 'all right' when clearly they don't give a damn. All *right*," he shouted, spittle flying. "All right *all right!*"

Missy froze, midstep.

"Always all right, always right, always. Why?" he asked, eyes feverish. "Why? Damn you, tell me why!"

Missy held her hands out slowly. "I'm sorry, I didn't mean to upset you—"

"Never mean. Never. Never!" he snarled. "Never mean what they say. Why say it? Why put it to words if the words are wrong? Why? *Why?* Tell me why!"

"I don't know," she said, keeping her voice level, hoping he wasn't going to have a seizure or worse. The way he was ranting, he was a candidate for a heart attack. "What are the right words?"

"Words, words. Empty words. Empty spaces." He wrapped his arms around himself and shuddered. "Empty inside."

That, Missy understood. "I wish I could be empty," she said wistfully. "There's too much inside of me. Even when I cut it away, it all comes back."

"Empty," he moaned. "I've lost my me. No one inside anymore. Empty spaces. Empty places. No me."

"I know who you are," Missy said. "You're Pestilence."

He stared at her, and something bright flickered behind his rheumy gaze, cutting through the feverish glaze. "Yes," he said. "Yes. Pestilence. The White Rider. Yes. That is who I am." He peered at her. "War?"

Her lips quirked in a brief smile. "So I'm told."

"I know you. No, not you. I know you, but not you." Fear skittered across his face. "Do I know you?"

"You know War," she said. "Me, I'm new. We haven't met before now."

He nodded slowly. "You're new. New. New is good. New beginnings. I had a beginning once. I had an ending, too, but I didn't like it." He grinned, revealing rotted teeth. "So I got a do-over."

Missy thought she was doing very well, considering the White Rider looked leprous and was more than halfway to crazy. "I got one too," she said. "Guess we're lucky."

"Not lucky. Sick. We're sick." He winked at her, the motion upsettingly intimate. "We're all sick, all of us. Dying a little more every day. The Pale Rider comes for us all. He comes." Pestilence bowed his head again, his shoulders shaking.

"Um," Missy said, fumbling. "What are you doing out here?"

"Here," he said, not looking up. "Here. What am I doing here? I shouldn't be here. I have responsibilities. Many responsibilities."

Remembering Famine's story about the Black Death, Missy said faintly, "I'm sure you do. Maybe you should, you know, get back to, um. What you do."

He looked up at her, held her gaze, and Missy understood that she was looking at the face of madness. It should have terrified her, but it only made her feel sad.

"I used to be a king. But my crown is tarnished," he said, touching the silver band over his eyebrows. It gleamed, as clean as his clothing, making his diseased face even more horrific to behold. "I stand naked before you."

A smell of earth and old parchment, and then a man's voice said from behind Missy, "It was the emperor's new clothes that were invisible. Yours are extremely old, and quite opaque. Which is good, as we're in mixed company."

Missy turned and there he was, Death, the moonlight captured in his hair. His smile softened the shock of his sudden appearance, but even so, she had one hand to her chest and told her heartbeat to slow down. "I swear," she said, "you need a bell around your neck."

"It would clash with my sweater. How are you tonight, Pestilence?"

When the other man didn't answer, Missy pivoted to find the White Rider cowering against the tree, his arms out to shield his face. Missy didn't recognize the gesture he was making with his hands, but she thought it might have been a ward against the evil eye. To Death, she quietly asked, "What's wrong with him?"

"Nothing," he murmured. "Other than everything. He is sickness incarnate. Sometimes, it gets the best of him. Like now."

"Too soon!" Pestilence shouted, his face still hidden. "Too soon! It's not time!"

"Easy now," said Death. "This isn't official. I was in the area, that's all."

Missy found herself lulled by his voice, by his smile—by his very presence. And his words weren't even directed at her. *The Horseman whisperer*, she thought, stifling a nervous giggle.

"Not time!" Pestilence screeched. Fast as flu, he scrambled to his feet. "Not now!"

Death called him by a different name, then, and reached out his hand. "Please," he said.

But Pestilence was already on his steed. With a panicked kick and a "Hyah!" the White Rider and his steed bolted onto the road, heading toward the horizon.

When the dust settled back to the ground, Missy frowned at Death. "You scared him."

"Happens sometimes." He shrugged. "Especially when he's having a bad spell."

She could still hear Pestilence's rambling words, could still feel his confusion and fear. "Is that what this was? A bad spell?"

"A poetic way to describe an inner battle. That's what lured you here. He was at war with his memory." In the darkness, Death's eyes looked almost silver. "Any sort of war will naturally attract you. But coming from one such as him? You were a moth to his flame. Don't take it personally. It's just part of being War."

"Oh." She paused, and before she could convince herself not to ask, she said, "If he's sick because he's sickness incarnate . . .

then what's going to happen to me because I'm war incarnate? Am I going to be at war with myself?"

"What makes you think that you're not already?"

Pestilence might have been gone, but she felt sick to her stomach. Was violence going to get the best of her the way Pestilence's illness had gotten the best of him?

And if it did, what did that mean for her?

Not brave enough to ask that question, she asked another. "What did he mean, 'not time'? Not time for what?"

"Pestilence is currently of the opinion that there is only one time when the Four Horsemen will gather." Death's voice was low, and cold, and filled with things that went bump in the night. "And that will be for the Last Ride."

Silence, as thick as blood.

"Of course, that's just his opinion," Death added. "It's been known to change, given his state of mind."

"So . . . is he right?" Missy asked.

Death smiled serenely. "He is mad but north-northwest."

Missy had no idea what to make of that. "You told me that *apocalypse* was just a word."

"I did. I also told you that words have power. As do actions." Death frowned into the distance. "I should go after him. Last time he was like this, swine flu tore through the place. And you should go home. It's late."

"But you're out now," she blurted. Death terrified her, yes—how could he not? But there was no denying that she was drawn to him, that she longed for his cold touch. Was that because War was Death's Handmaiden? Or was it because she, Missy Miller, enjoyed the way his eyes shone as if he had a million secrets? "And Pestilence is out now. Why shouldn't I be out now?"

He glanced at her, arching his brow. "I've been doing this for a long time. And unlike some, I'm not going through an identity crisis."

Missy crossed her arms and dug in her heels. "You gave me the Sword for a reason. I should be using it."

"I did," he said, rewarding her with a magnificent smile. "And you are."

She tried to ignore the way that smile sped up her heart and made her knees rubbery. She failed spectacularly.

"Good night, Melissa Miller." He bowed, low enough for his too-long blond hair to cascade over his face and hide his smile.

"Good night," she whispered, but he was already gone.

Missy stared at the spot he had been for a long, long time. Finally, she turned to Ares. "Come on," she said. "Let's go home."

Chapter 14

Sunday mornings in the Miller house meant oversize breakfasts and weekly planning, and this Sunday was no different. As everyone filled a plate with scrambled eggs, bacon, and toast, Missy's mother had the refrigerator calendar ready to go, highlighters lined up like soldiers. Scheduling was serious business. Missy thought her mother would have been an excellent wedding planner.

Actually, Missy was amazed she could think at all. There was exhaustion, and then there was absolutely wrecked: the sort of fatigue that vibrates in the marrow of your bones and makes you feel like you're dragging a thousand pounds. Missy, so wrecked that junkyards would have begged her for scrap metal, took a sip of coffee and hoped that *this* sip would be the one that shook her out of her near coma. She had to muddle through breakfast. Somehow. She let out a jaw-cracking yawn and nearly spilled her coffee. Blinking hard, she scrubbed the sleep from her eyes. If she passed out in her eggs, Sue would never let her hear the end of it.

But then, her sister was oddly quiet. As Missy sipped, she glanced at Sue, catching her in the act of glaring sullenly at her. Sue's nostrils flared, and then she abruptly looked away, as if the platter of buttered toast were of the utmost interest.

Whatever. As long as Sue sulked quietly, all was right with the world.

"Ready," her mother declared. "Who's kicking it off?"

Missy managed not to roll her eyes. Her dad would go first, as he did every Sunday brunch. Then her mom. Then it would be her turn, and Sue, ever the darling baby girl, would go last. That's where the best was, right? And that's where the fabled nice guys were. Sue would get the nice guy and make their parents blissfully happy, and Missy would be left to fawn over Death—who was many things, but definitely not a nice guy.

No, not a guy at all. A concept in a rock god's clothing.

Missy's mouth twitched into a smile as she imagined Death running his long, cold fingers over her, making music on her body. Would his kisses be cold? Or would they be hot enough to burn away her fears, to turn her dead face to ash and reveal her soul to the world?

Her father started talking, and that got her to stop thinking about Death (especially about doing things with Death that would have made her parents faint). Missy feigned interest as her dad explained in painstaking detail why he'd be working late every night, all thanks to the office launch in two weeks. Next up: her mom, all fired up about a big meeting with company muckity-mucks on Tuesday morning. The girls would have to make their own dinners on Monday night, said Mom, because she would be at the office until God only knew when.

In other words, Missy and Sue would be alone tomorrow night. The unspoken "Don't destroy the house" was very clear. The sisters made the appropriate "You can trust us" noises.

The next ten minutes were all about their parents getting into How Important their work was, and how much it meant to them that the girls understood just what was at stake. *What's to understand?* Missy wondered as she smiled blandly and nibbled a slice of bacon. Her parents worked hard. They succeeded. She got it. She didn't know why they always seemed so apologetic, even when they were practically glowing with accomplishment. That was just stupid. Do what you need to do, and don't feel bad about it.

Then again, it would be nice if her folks had time to see her at one of her games.

When it was her turn, Missy ran down her list quickly: soccer practice after school every day except Tuesday; games on Tuesday and Saturday; tests scattered throughout the week.

"You should think about doing some volunteer work," her father said as he poured a glass of orange juice. "That will look good when it's time to apply for college."

"Dad's right," said her mother, highlighting like crazy. "Find something you're passionate about and get involved."

"Like the teen crisis help line," her sister said, sweet enough to send a diabetic into shock. "I can't think of anyone who can relate to troubled teens better than you, sis." Her smile said "I care" and her eyes said "Drop dead." It was quite the trick.

Missy saluted Sue with her coffee cup, making sure to leave her middle finger extended just enough for Sue to see it.

"What a marvelous idea!" That was her father, terribly pleased.

"Absolutely," crowed her mother. "Melissa, you'd be a natural. Terrific suggestion, Susan."

Sue grinned as if she'd won a shopping spree at her favorite shoe store.

Missy smiled tightly and thought of what it would feel like to kill Sue. Slowly. "I'll think about it."

Then it was her sister's turn to wow everyone with her jam-packed schedule for the week. Missy stopped listening once Sue started babbling about a bake sale to raise money for Cheer. As if any of the cheerleaders dared to eat anything with carbs in it.

SHEEP, War whispered. *LISTEN TO IT BLEAT*.

Missy finished her breakfast and smiled at her sister, thinking about taking the Sword and carving away Sue's life. The lies, first—the plastic face she presented to the world (nothing at all like Missy's own dead face), the one that showed her as perky and cute and a team player. Then the intentions: the surface goals of good grades and being a dutiful daughter, baring her true self to the world. Her sister would scream over getting dirty. She would scream out of indignation.

And then, when the steel cut deep, she would simply scream.

Missy sipped her coffee, and smiled, and pretended to listen to her sister as War whispered in her mind.

||||||

"Here."

On her bed, Missy looked up from her pre-calc textbook to see Sue waving a piece of paper in front of her. "Ever hear of knocking?"

"Ever hear of closing your door if you want privacy?"

"Get that out of my face." She slapped at the paper, but Sue kept holding it, shoving it right at her. Glaring at her sister, Missy plucked it out of Sue's hand. It was a phone number scrawled on loose-leaf paper.

"That's the local teen crisis hot line," Sue said. "You should call them."

Missy, safe behind her dead face, drilled her gaze through her sister. Blood should have spattered on the door. "I said I'd think about it. I don't know if I have time for volunteer work."

"Who's talking about a job?"

Anger throbbed behind Missy's eyes.

Sue crossed her arms and thrust out her hip, playing at indignation, and her mouth pulled down in a pout. "Call them. Maybe they can talk sense into you."

"I'm fine," Missy said, voice flat.

Her sister moved faster than Missy would have guessed possible—one second she was standing over the bed, the next she had Missy's right arm in her hand and was pushing back the shirtsleeve.

"You're *not* fine," Sue hissed, spitting fury. "You look like you ran into a lawn mower."

Missy yanked her arm away, her head pounding in a drum solo. She wanted to scream, to hide, to shove her fists against the wall until her bones shattered. She needed to take her razor and cut herself until all she felt was sting and bliss, sting and bliss. She had to atone for her sins in blood. Blood washed it all away and left her clean. Pure.

Taking a deep breath, she shoved everything into the glass jar of her heart, pushing it all down before she did or said something she would regret.

Because oh, she wanted to do something. She wanted to grab Sue by her hair and slam her face against the wall until her features were nothing but a red, lumpy blur. She wanted to peel away those judgmental eyes and yank out her sharp tongue. She wanted to hit her, and hit her, and hit her until her sister's body was little more than tenderized meat.

YOU COULD, War murmured. *YOU COULD DO IT SO EASILY.*

Sue was staring at her as if she were a rabid dog that had crapped on the carpet—her eyes brimmed with disgust and fear and caution, and something else, too, something that Missy couldn't pinpoint.

HURT HER.

Sue sniffed loudly. "Get some help. You think I want to be the sister of an emo cutter freak?"

Control, Missy told herself, breathing deeply. *Control.* She sealed the glass jar and tucked it away. Her dead face in position, she leveled a blank gaze at her sister. "I don't give a damn what you want. Get out of my room."

Sue's shoulders tensed. "Not until you promise to call the hot line."

"Fine." Missy sat up, dropping her textbook onto the bed. Enough, and more than enough. She was a Horseman of the damn Apocalypse. She didn't have to sit in her room and take crap from her little sister. She stood up, forcing Sue to take a step backward. "You stay," Missy said. "I'm going downstairs."

As she walked past Sue, Missy bumped her—a nudge of her shoulders, just enough to push her sister aside. She didn't have to; there was plenty of room to have maneuvered around her. But she had wanted to. Just a little bump, a push, a quiet statement that warned her sister not to ignore her. Actions, after all, spoke louder than words.

And oh, that action had felt *good.*

Missy was at her bedroom door when Sue shoved her, hard, on her back. Missy staggered, her arms wide, and for a crystalline second she hung on the precipice, startled, poised to fall.

Missy reached out, and War took hold. An instant later, she planted her feet, two cushioned thumps on the carpet. Hunched forward, knees bent, she stood there, breathing heavily as her vision tunneled to two points of red.

Her sister *pushed* her. In *her own room.*

Hairline cracks sprouted along the glass jar, thorn-sharp.

"Who the hell do you think you are?" Sue shouted. "You don't bump me! You don't walk away and *bump* me!"

The cracks spread, lattice-like, until they covered the jar.

"You hear me, freak? I'm talking to you!"

The jar shattered, and Missy let the Red pull her under.

HURT HER, War crooned, the voice hypnotic, insistent. HURT HER BADLY.

Slowly, Missy pivoted until she was facing Sue. She smiled, showing teeth. It was the smile of whimsical murder, of gleeful slaughter.

Her sister's face went ghost white.

"Get out of my room," Missy said very, very softly. "Or I'll hurt you. Badly."

Sue ran. A moment later, a bedroom door slammed shut. On the heels of that, their mother's voice called out, scolding fiercely about slamming doors.

Missy's smile twisted into something cruel as she silently closed her bedroom door. Too easy. For all of her attitude, Sue was just a Barbie trying to be a Bratz doll. Sue had no urge to hurt anyone, to strip away falsehoods and leave the truth naked and bleeding. Violence was just a word to people like her. When it was time for fighting, they were the first to crumple.

SHEEP, War laughed. THEY'RE SHEEP. EASILY LED. EASILY FRIGHTENED.

Sue had definitely been frightened. Her fear had filled Missy's nostrils, had given her a sugar rush.

FEAR IS SWEET, War agreed. BUT TERROR IS ADDICTIVE.

That made Missy pause, and the smile slipped from her face. Did she want her sister terrified of her?

OF COURSE YOU DO.

No, she didn't. So why was her fist clenched so tight that it was trembling? Why did she want to lash out and break whatever was in her way?

Missy hugged herself, told herself that this fury would pass, that it wasn't filling her and spilling out of her pores. That she could handle it.

That she didn't need the blade.

BUT YOU DO, said War.

Missy closed her eyes and saw Sue's horror-stricken face. She bit her lip and imagined her hands stained with Sue's blood.

No, she thought, desperate. No. This isn't me.

BUT IT CAN BE, War said. WE CAN BLEED THE WORLD DRY.

And the truly horrific thing was, Missy wanted to do exactly that.

Her eyes popped open and she lunged to her closet. No more thinking; no more whisperings and urges and thoughts she couldn't control. She yanked the door open. No more visions of Red drowning the world as she held her Sword aloft. Missy grabbed her lockbox and fumbled it open.

No more words.

She took out her razor and pulled back her sleeve and slashed a line in the bend of her elbow. And she did it again. And again. She did it until the anger bled out and her arm was dripping and numb and her hand shook so much that the razor slipped

from her fingers. It landed on the carpeted floor with a muffled thud.

SEE? War whispered. *YOU DO NEED THE BLADE.*

Sobbing, Missy pressed her sleeve against the hungry wounds.
She waited for the small bit of serenity to come over her, to wrap
her in strong arms and rock her until everything was calm.

She waited a long, long time.

Finally, she let out a miserable sigh and began to clean up.

CHAPTER 15

After a session with her razor, Missy usually felt peaceful. At the very least, she became more focused, able to handle the overwhelming emotions and thoughts that had driven her to the blade. Sometimes, that sense of peace would extend into something almost rapturous and she'd feel as if she had seen the face of God. Other times, she was left with a simple feeling of quiet, of warmth and solace.

This was the first time she had ever felt bleak.

She rocked on her bedroom floor, the lights off, the door closed, her arms wrapped around her knees. A gray lump sat in her stomach, a wretched stone of guilt that crushed any semblance of peace. She had wandered out of the land of Too Much and set up camp in Emptyville. Tumbleweeds blew in her chest, and she breathed the dust of abandoned buildings.

She had wanted to hurt her sister. And more than hurt—she had wanted to feel her sister's face beneath her fist, bruise her knuckles on her sister's bones. She had wanted to draw the Sword and make her sister scream. She had wanted that so very much.

She didn't know who she was anymore.

Melissa Miller rocked, alone in the dark. And she despaired.

At the dinner table, Missy and Sue didn't speak to each other. Missy, for that matter, didn't speak at all. Their parents chatted for a bit as they served huge slices of steaming pizza out of the box, while the girls sat in strained silence. But after ten minutes of discussing various work-related projects, their father tried to draw Missy and Sue into the conversation. Neither sister complied. Finally, he asked them why they were, as he put it, "in a snit." Sue pointedly refused to answer; she picked at the vegetables coating her slice of pizza, took sips of water, and didn't look Missy in the eye. For her part, Missy sat slumped in her high-backed chair and stared at the cooling food on her plate.

"Girls," their dad said, "come on. Talk it out."

No response.

"I'll help negotiate the Miller Peace Accords," he said gamely.

Nothing, not even an eyeroll from either sister.

Their mother sighed as she reached for another slice. "Look, we understand that sisters sometimes need to be mad at each other." She leveled a significant look at her daughters. "But I wish it wouldn't be at the dinner table."

Missy knew a cue when she heard one. She scraped her chair back and grabbed her plate.

"Melissa," her mom warned. "You weren't excused."

"You don't like how I'm acting at the table. So I'm going out." Missy marched out of the dining room before her shocked mother could respond. She dumped her uneaten pizza into the trash and shoved on her sneakers. As she walked through the living room, she heard her sister say, "She's out of control."

If her parents had any reply, it was cut off when Missy slammed the front door.

She walked without purpose, her feet dragging. It wasn't until she felt a gentle bump—so very unlike her sister's two-handed shove—that she realized Ares was walking behind her. She turned to face the warhorse, and she managed a smile as it nuzzled against her shoulder.

"Hey," she said, scratching behind its ears. "Hey there." She swallowed thickly. "You don't have to keep me company. I'm okay."

The warhorse's ears flickered.

"Really, I am."

The red horse nuzzled her again. Its intention was clear: it wasn't leaving her side.

"You're a good steed," she said, her voice breaking. She threw her arms around Ares' neck. "The best," she whispered, hugging tightly.

They stood there for a time, a girl and a horse, each taking comfort from the other's presence. And then the girl climbed up onto the horse's back and the two went out into the night.

||||||

They moved among the humans, invisible, weaving through their lives. Missy hefted the Sword, but instead of urging people to violence she sliced through their pain, working as she had just yesterday in a desert land. She bled them, and hope closed their wounds. Agonies—over money, over love, over all the things that make people doubt and hate themselves— slowly eased from Missy's steely touch. Small wars ended, if only for a little while. Tomorrow, people might once again lash out at one another, might allow their wants to dictate their needs. But for tonight, they settled down, content with their lot. For tonight, peace reigned.

But even as she cut away the red lines of fury that kept people in a stranglehold, Missy herself remained trapped in a quagmire of gray.

Eventually, Missy tired of wielding the Sword, so the war-horse brought her home. She thanked her steed for the company and gave it a farewell pat. And then she went inside her house.

Her father told her she was grounded. Missy didn't care.

Her mother told her she could talk to her, that she could say anything. Missy didn't care.

Sue avoided her. Missy didn't care.

Alone once more in her room, Missy stripped off her clothes and sat beneath the black-and-white poster of Marilyn Monroe and James Dean that hung on her closet door, and she ran the pads of her thumbs over the scars on her arms, her belly, her legs. Tomorrow was Monday, and she'd have to face the aftermath of Adam's public betrayal.

And she didn't care.

War can be a tragedy, said a small, still voice. *But you could be something more.*

She let out a bitter laugh. How could she be something more when she didn't even know who she was?

The Sword reverberated in her mind, clanging like a death knell. *YOU'RE WAR.*

Melissa Miller wanted to cry, but the tears wouldn't come.

MONDAY

CHAPTER 16

On Monday, Missy woke before dawn. She sat at the edge of her bed for a minute, listening for the purr of a dead cat. But Graygirl was long gone, and if there were such things as ghosts, hers chose not to make an appearance. Missy stared down at her hands on her lap, tried to remember the feeling of a furry body between them—how Graygirl's tongue would sandpaper the webbing of skin between Missy's thumb and index finger. But all she could feel was the memory of the cat's empty body sagging against her arms, and she heard a final pleading cry echo until it was lost in the sounds of her breathing.

You have blood on your hands.

Yes, she surely did.

With a sigh, she stood up and began her school-morning routine. She opened her closet and carefully selected her clothing, all black, and she went to her jewelry box and plucked out her accessories, all silver, and she arranged them all on her bed as if they were weapons.

Today, she told herself, *is just another Monday.*

She went to the bathroom and did her business, then proceeded to take an excruciatingly hot shower. She shampooed and conditioned; she scrubbed her body with soap. She took her time with the pink disposable razor, cutting paths through the stubble on her legs, her bikini area, her armpits. She stood under the spray and didn't wince as the hot water rained on her

face. She closed her eyes and traced her fingers over her scars,
reading the raised and puckered skin as if it were Braille, telling
the story of her pain.

All part of the routine. All part of the motions of her life.

Today is just another Monday.

Clean, she dried off and polished her teeth until they
gleamed. She couldn't see her reflection in the steam-fogged
mirror. She didn't mind. She spat into the sink and didn't rinse
her mouth. Peppermint on her tongue, she turned off the light
and went back to her bedroom.

She dressed in the dark.

She hadn't checked her e-mail messages at all. She'd deleted all
texts and voice mails and video clips from her phone yesterday
without looking at them. She didn't turn her phone on this morning. She made sure not to put it in her pocket or her backpack.

. . . just another Monday.

As she armed herself with jewelry, light began to slip under
her windowshade. In the soft gray of her room, Missy slowly
arranged her makeup on top of her dresser. And then it was
time to paint her dead face.

By the time her sister's door opened and Sue was lumbering
to the bathroom, Missy had finished with her warpaint and was
spiking her hair.

. . . another Monday.

Twenty minutes later, Missy grabbed her backpack and her
soccer gear and walked out of her room just as Sue left the bathroom. The two sisters stared at each other, their unspoken words
screaming in the silence between them. Finally, Sue turned
around and went back into the bathroom. The door shut with a
soft click.

Missy tried to feel something, *anything* about her sister, but the broken glass jar of her heart was now a ghost town. Empty, she headed downstairs. Once her boots were on her feet, she exited, stage right. She made sure not to slam the front door.

Just another Monday. If she said it to herself enough times, maybe she'd even believe it.

||||||

The red steed watched its mistress leave the house. It wanted to go to her, but a pale hand commanded it to remain still.

"Some things," said Death, "we have to do alone."

||||||

For a while, it looked like she was going to make it.

Missy avoided the other students as best she could. Morning classes themselves weren't a problem, other than the whispers behind the teachers' backs and the occasional glances her way. She was used to that—she'd had months and months of people judging her for the way she looked—so she just focused on her schoolwork and pretended everything was normal.

Navigating the hallways was a little trickier, but her dead face shielded her as she marched around people clustering by their lockers. She heard the laughter, of course; turning a blind eye didn't miraculously make her deaf. But Missy had lots of practice at ignoring her so-called peers as they attempted to display sarcastic wit. They mocked her, but she was the queen of winter, and she chose not to acknowledge their petty remarks. They were beneath her.

SHOW THEM YOUR STRENGTH, War whispered. *BE BRUTAL.*

Missy ignored that too. She was a veteran of the battle of high school; War's advice was superfluous. She kept her Sword sheathed.

After third period, she went to her locker to exchange her morning books for her afternoon workload. When she shut the door, Adam was grinning down at her. Behind him, his entourage capered and jeered their warning shots.

"For you, baby," Adam said, flinging her stolen panties at her. The underwear bounced off her chest and fell to the floor.

The entourage of Matts and jocks all cracked up.

That's when Missy smashed the smug movie-star grin off Adam's face. She felt his eyes pop as she dug her fingers into his sockets. She smelled his pain, his fear, the acrid stench of urine in his pants. She heard the boys' laughter stutter and die. She hit him again, and again, her knuckles now raw and bloody. She hit him until his grin was a memory and his teeth rattled on the ground. When someone wrestled her off of him, she kicked him twice in the groin. "For you!" she screamed as they pulled her away. "For *you,* baby! All for you!"

And over it all, she heard War's murmur of approval.

Missy blinked, and Adam was still grinning at her, daring her to do something.

DO IT, War urged. *BREAK HIS SPIRIT. BREAK HIS SKULL. LEAVE YOUR MARK ON HIM SO HE'LL NEVER FORGET YOU. HURT HIM!*

On the floor, her underwear from Friday night lay crumpled at her feet.

She wanted to draw the Sword and let it kiss his skin. She wanted to part his flesh with her steel and let his blood spatter the linoleum of the hallway. She wanted that more than she had ever wanted, needed, to take a razor to her body.

A toddler chased a soccer ball, his delighted squeals echoing in Missy's ears.

She forced herself to smile. "Keep it," she told Adam. "I know how you like to wear it."

With that parting shot, she retreated, leaving Adam and his groupies to insult her, loudly and creatively. Her heart jack-hammered in her chest, and she thought she was going to throw up. Instead of heading toward the cafeteria, she beelined it to the library. Seeing Adam had made her lose her appetite. Besides, she told herself, she needed the time to finish studying for her pre-calc test.

When the bell rang, she joined the stream of students heading to their fifth-period classes. A number of them, fresh from the lunchroom, bombarded her with clucking sounds. *Queen of winter*, Missy reminded herself, grinding her teeth. She'd survived Adam. She could get through the rest of the day.

Just outside of her math class, Trudy, Jenna, and two other soccer girls surrounded her. Jenna draped her arm over Missy's shoulders, and Trudy grinned in her face. "Missed you at lunch," Trudy said.

"Guess that's where you get your name, huh, Missy?" Jenna laughed.

"Clever," Missy said, standing rigid. "You think of that all by yourself?"

"We have a present for you," Trudy said.

"Picked it out special," Jenna added.

This was just her day of presents, wasn't it? *Get it over with. Just take it and move past it.* She could do it.

One of the other girls shoved a paper bag at Missy. "For your habit," she said, giggling.

Missy stared hard at the girl as she took the bag. She thought about how easy it would be to rip those gaudy earrings off her ears, wondered if the lobes would bleed.

THEY WOULD, War said. AND SHE'D HAVE SCARS FOR THE REST OF HER LIFE. LIKE YOU.

Inside the bag was a package of disposable razors.

"Oh my God," said a passing boy, who pulled away from his buddies to get into Missy's space. "It's you, it's really you!" He grinned hugely, and Missy smelled garlic on his breath. "I've seen *all* of your movies."

The soccer girls cackled.

Her throat closed up. This was so much worse than Adam. Him, she knew. But this boy? He was nameless. He was just a guy, and he'd seen her naked. He was just a no one, but he knew her scars intimately.

KILL THEM, War whispered.

Missy squeezed her eyes shut.

"Aw, look. She's going to cry."

"Tell me it was a body double," said one of the other, equally nameless boys. "No way that was her. Girl on the video was hot."

"Look at her," a third guy said, "all covered up like that. Girl I saw had no problem showing skin."

Someone grabbed her arm and tried to shove up her sleeve. Missy's eyes snapped open as she wrenched her arm away. "Get your hands off me!"

"So touchy," said one of the boys.

"So feely," said another, laughing. "I hear you put out if the money's right. How much is it to get laid by a bona-fide movie star?"

"Cut-rate prices, I bet," said the first boy.

The soccer girls shrieked laughter. "Missy," Trudy said, "you're such a slut!"

"Cutterslut," said Jenna smugly, right before the bell rang.

KILL THEM ALL, War crooned.

Missy shut her eyes again and told herself to breathe, just breathe.

She was still standing outside of class, holding a bag filled with disposable razors, when her teacher told her to come in for the test. She took her seat and took her test, but all she wrote in the answer booklet was "You don't know me," again and again and again.

She floated in a gray funk during sixth-period chemistry. Around her, other students murmured and snickered, but they were background noise. Not even the Sword's whisperings could cut through her malaise. Erica tried to get her to talk, to roll her eyes and make caustic remarks, but Missy couldn't hear her. The instructor droned, and the students murmured, and Missy floated.

By the end of class, Missy snapped out of it. Yes, Adam had ruined her and everyone had laughed. Yes, she was the butt of the joke, a complete laughingstock. But she would get through this. She had soccer. She had the Sword. She was more than just a high school loser. She smiled at Erica and told her she was okay. Erica didn't believe her, but the bell was ringing and it was time to move on to seventh period. For Missy, it was time for gym.

In the locker room, she exchanged her skirt and boots for cutoffs and sneakers. As she pulled off her jewelry, she thought that all things considered, today hadn't gone too badly. She had to keep her head down, that was all. She made sure her backpack, soccer gear, and clothing were secure in her locker, and then she went into the gym, thinking that she could make it through her classes as long as she focused. And she could make it through the hallways as long as she ignored the idiots. Don't rise to the bait. That was key.

She could make it through the rest of junior year, and Adam be damned.

The mixed-grade upperclassmen PE class was her favorite, partially because the girls' varsity soccer coach was the instructor and partially because they were up to the volleyball unit and Missy loved being on the court. Her serves were all right, but she really got height in her jumps, and her spikes were sheer poetry: fluid rage, pinpoint violence. Bella, who was the student PE leader for the day, nodded at her before she started leading the class through a warm-up routine. Missy followed along, stretching in time to Bella's counts, already thinking about bumps and sets.

"Missy."

She looked up to see the coach standing by the office door, motioning her inside. Missy scrambled to her feet and jogged over. Once inside, the coach told her to shut the door. Missy did so.

The coach leaned against her desk, the casual pose belied by her serious face. "You did well on Saturday," she said.

Missy blushed beneath her dead face; the coach wasn't known for her praise. "Thanks."

"You made a few mistakes, but everyone does the first time. With more time on the field, you'd be a fearsome goalkeeper."

Fearsome. Oh, she did so like the sound of that. A hesitant smile crept over her face, teasing her lips, flickering in her eyes. "Really?"

"Really. Which makes this conversation all the more difficult. Are you a cutter?"

Missy's smile froze. "Excuse me?"

"Are you a cutter, Missy?" The coach didn't move, but something about her posture changed—her shoulders were more rigid, her jaw tighter. "Do you take a razor and make yourself bleed?"

Missy's heart galloped in her chest. Of all the things she had expected today, being confronted by a teacher hadn't made the list. She floundered, her mouth gaping as Outrage and Horror battled for dominance. She stammered, "Wh-Who's saying that?"

"The who doesn't matter." A moment of tension, palpable, almost painful. "I need to know if it's true. Is it true, Missy?"

Horror grabbed Outrage in a headlock and choked it down. Blushing again, this time from shame, Missy looked away. She wanted to lie; she wanted to scream, to drum her fists against the wall, to force Adam and Trudy and Sue and everyone who had led her to this moment here in this tiny office to crash to their knees and kiss the dirt and beg for forgiveness; she wanted to admit the truth, that she had Bic-marks for birthmarks all over her arms and legs and stomach; she wanted absolution.

Missy wanted all of that, and none of that, so she said nothing and desperately wished this wasn't happening. She swallowed the lump in her throat, and it was bitter.

A minute passed. Then another.

"Did something happen?" her coach asked softly. "When you were a kid, maybe? Someone do something to you they shouldn't have?"

Adam had ravaged her trust and left it broken and dying on the curb. But Missy had been cutting before Adam had ever asked her out. She whispered, "No."

Harsher now: "You on drugs?"

"No," Missy rasped. "Never."

A pause. "You doing it because it's cool?"

Fury blew through Missy, making her blood boil. Out of all the ways she would have described cutting, "cool" wasn't even close. "*No.*"

"Do your parents know?"

Missy finally met her coach's eyes. "No."

Another minute passed.

"You should talk to the guidance counselor," said the coach. "Or make an appointment with a psychologist, someone not at school. What you're doing to yourself is bad. You know that, don't you?"

Grinding her teeth, Missy nodded curtly.

The coach nodded grimly. "Good. Maybe next year, we can give soccer another shot."

Blinking, Missy said, "What . . . ?"

"You're off the team, Missy." The coach's eyes glittered like diamond chips—bright, hard, cutting. "At best, you're a bad influence on the other girls. At worst, soccer's high pressure, especially for the goalkeeper. I won't contribute to your bad habit."

Sucker-punched, Missy staggered back. Tears burned her eyes. She tried to speak, but all she managed was a strangled "Please."

"Stop being stupid," said the coach, "and I'll let you try out for the team next year."

Blood roared in Missy's ears, slammed behind her eyes with every wild thump of her heart. A balloon expanded in her chest, squeezing her empty heart and making it impossible for her to breathe.

She had to get out.

Missy whirled and jerked the door open. The coach might have said something else, but Missy was too far gone to hear it. She tore past Bella, past the other girls in the gym. She raced out of the locker room, not stopping to get her things. She fled down the hallway to the school's back exit and bolted out the door.

At the corner, she sank to her knees and wrapped her arms over her head.

THEY WILL ALL BETRAY YOU, War said.

And they would. Whether it was her teachers or her friends or her family, they would all betray her. Maybe it would be couched in helpful terms, and maybe their faces would be brimming with sympathy. But in the end, they would all let her down.

They would all cut her down.

They would all slap labels on her and spoon-feed her appropriate words, wipe her mouth with their expectations. They would wind her up and make her dance, and when they were done they'd put her away. They would keep doing it and doing it, until she was nothing more than a shell, a skin, something to slip on and slip off and tuck in at the corners.

They would . . . unless she stopped them.

Yes, she thought, breathing heavily. She could stop them. All of them. She could take the Sword and cut through all the garbage, all the falsehoods and plastic smiles, all the platitudes and nonsense, cut through it all and leave the truth bleeding and naked. She could force people to see themselves for what they really were, force them to deal with the ugliness of the real world.

She could.

She should.

Melissa Miller screwed her eyes shut and threw her arms wide, her mouth open in a piercing scream. The scream twisted into a cruel laugh, one that echoed with kicked-down doors and midnight raids.

A moment later, War opened her eyes.

And she grinned.

CHAPTER 17

WAR

THE WORLD IS A WOUND AND I WILL CAUTERIZE IT.

PEOPLE ARE VERMIN AND I WILL EXTERMINATE THEM.

THE STRONG ARE THE WORTHY; THROUGH BLOOD, I WILL LEAD THEM TO SALVATION.

I COME.

HEAR MY BATTLE CRY AND DESPAIR.

MISSY

I see a woman in red who looks like me but isn't me.

She wields a weapon the way a hero holds a heroine—with reverence, with passion, maybe even with love.

She radiates strength like heat off a skillet; she is the epitome of power.

She is everything I am not.

I want to hate her. I want to run from her. But instead I hide from the world and hate only myself.

Hatred is easy because, as they say, practice makes perfect.

WAR

PEOPLE WILL CRY FOR MERCY, BUT I HAVE NONE.

THE RICH WILL SHIELD THEMSELVES WITH MONEY, BUT MY SWORD WILL CUT THROUGH PAPER AND GOLD AND FLESH.

THE POOR WILL FIGHT WITH DESPERATION, AND I WILL LAUGH, AMUSED.

THE WORLD WILL ONCE AGAIN COWER IN THE DARK, WITH ONLY THE GLEAM OF STEEL FOR ITS LIGHT.

RUN TO ME OR RUN FROM ME; EITHER WAY, I WILL CUT YOU DOWN.

THIS IS THE PROMISE OF WAR.

MISSY

She is the sun; looking at her too long will surely blind me. So I will hide my face in my hands as she advances. I will cower in the dark as she destroys everything, starting with . . .

. . . my school?

WAR

ADULTS DESERVE NO MORE RESPECT THAN THE WORMS BENEATH THE EARTH; THEIR WISDOM AND EXPERIENCE WILL NOT SAVE THEM.

CHILDREN WILL SCREAM AND THEIR INNOCENCE WILL DIE; THEIR YOUTH AND POTENTIAL WILL NOT SAVE THEM.

I WILL DELIVER THEIR DEATH KNELLS AND LAY THEIR BODIES AT THE FEET OF THE PALE RIDER.

THE WORLD WILL END WITH NEITHER A BANG NOR A WHIMPER, BUT WITH BLOOD.

IN THE END, IT'S ALWAYS BLOOD.

MISSY

Every step she takes booms like thunder.

I come to my feet as she approaches the building—that dread

institution of audacity and hormones, all wrapped in a pretty box and topped with a diploma.

Adam is in there.

Adam and the Matts and Jenna and Trudy and everyone I despise, even my sister. Especially my sister. They're in there and they're going to die.

Bella is in there. Erica too. And so many others. Thousands of people, including my sister. Especially my sister.

I feel pressure growing in me, filling me until I'm going to burst.

WAR

I raise my Sword high.

The time has come for slaughter.

MISSY

She reaches the stairs that will take her inside the school, my school, and I shout a word, one small word that freezes her in place.

And then she turns, slowly, her red eyes flashing like heat lightning.

God, I am completely terrified, so scared that I feel like I'm dying. But deeper than the terror is my rage.

She wants to hurt everyone in my school, *everyone*, saint and sinner alike, wants to shred them like confetti and toss their souls upon the wind.

I plant my feet and stare her in the eye as I say it again, the one small word that changes everything:

No.

CHAPTER 18

She stood on the steps to the high school: a sixteen-year-old girl who housed the eternal spirit of aggression. Most people passing by, if they saw her at all, would have thought she was odd, perhaps due to the clothing she wore and the makeup on her face. They would not have seen the red glow to her eyes, or the way hundreds of cuts on her arms and legs and stomach glowed like magic runes. They would not have seen the gleaming Sword in her hand, lifted high as if to split the sky.

Death, of course, wasn't most people.

Whistling, he took a seat at the top of the steps. His horse stood sentry behind him, as immobile as the marble columns on either side of the large front door. Next to the pale steed, the warhorse waited just as quietly, though its body trembled with trapped fury. Death took it in good cheer; the steeds, after all, reflected their Riders—and War was not known for patience.

Humming now, Death watched what was happening on the bottom steps. School would be letting out shortly, but he wasn't concerned.

Either way, the battle would be over all too soon.

||||||

They stood on the battlefield of Missy's mind: a sixteen-year-old girl and the eternal spirit of aggression. Around them, reds and oranges burned the sky in a sunset of fire, and smoke drifted lazily, stinging Missy's nostrils with the smells of singed hair and charred flesh. A soccer field yawned beneath them, the dead grass affixed with sickly white lines. At either end of the field was a goal, the posts and netting as red as sin.

War and Missy faced each other in the center circle. The knight shone brightly, the silver-plated armor winking with crimson mesh at the joints. A scarlet plume crested her helm, stabbing the air and making the sky bleed. Within the shadows of her faceguard, her eyes gleamed wetly, murderously.

Missy bounced on her heels, the teeth of her cleats digging into the stiff grass. Her goalie uniform was comfortable, familiar, but how would it help her now? Sure, her leather gloves would keep her hands from getting chopped up, and her shin guards would protect her legs. But a goalkeeper was no match for a knight.

Just because you're a goalie, Bella whispered, *doesn't mean you can't be shrewd.*

Shrewd. Yeah, that'll stop a fistful of metal. Adrenaline surged through Missy, making her blood sing and her feet want to move, to run—far away, and fast.

Don't be afraid, Bella said. *Be confident.*

Confident. Right. Missy held her ground and pretended she wasn't about to pee out of sheer fright.

"Who are you, girl, to tell me no?"

War's voice—no longer a whisper in Missy's head—was a thing of nightmares. It was the voice of the monster in the closet, of the bogeyman under the bed. It was the sound of fury and madness incarnate. It was a voice cultivated to inspire terror.

Except it pushed Missy so far past terror that she found herself absurdly calm. Was it possible to be scared to a point at which you weren't stopped by the fear? She stood tall and replied, "I am Melissa Miller. And I won't let you destroy my school."

The Red Rider threw back her head and laughed, her bellowing chortles echoing in the hazy air. "YOU LET ME IN," said War. "YOU HEARD THE SONG OF THE SWORD AND YOU DANCED TO ITS TUNE. YOU CAN'T TELL ME NO."

"Just did," Missy said.

"YOUR ARGUMENT FALLS ON DEAF EARS." Though her face was hidden within the helm, her smile was all too clear in her voice. "I AM THE RUMBLE OF VOLCANOES WAKING AFTER SLEEP. I AM THE PRESS OF THE BUTTON THAT LAUNCHES THE MISSILES. AND YOU? YOU'RE JUST A GIRL."

Missy remembered the cold touch of gentle fingers on her cheek, and she grinned. "I'm just a girl who wields your Sword."

|||||||

A black horse joined the others. It stood as far from the red steed as possible, and it contented itself by nibbling the weeds at the edges of the steps. The warhorse snorted, but it wouldn't attack the black, not with the pale steed standing between them.

Famine took a seat to the right of Death and watched the girl at the bottom of the stairs. After a moment, the Black Rider sighed. "I should have killed her when I had the chance."

Death chuckled. "And where would have been the fun in that?"

||||||

Missy crossed her hand to her hip, ready to draw the Sword and deal some serious pain to the hulking knight—but the weapon wouldn't come out. It stayed in its sheath, wherever the hell *that* was.

"IDIOT," War sneered. "I *AM* THE SWORD."

Well, that put a damper on her plan.

Missy stopped herself from whimpering, but she couldn't stop the sweat from popping on her brow. How was she supposed to face down War if she didn't have a weapon?

Intimidate the hell out of your opponent, Bella urged.

Missy was fairly certain Bella would have taken one look at War and fainted dead away.

"IT IS TIME FOR ME TO RIDE, LITTLE GIRL," War rumbled. "STAY OUT OF MY WAY, OR DIE WITH THE OTHERS. IT MAKES NO MATTER TO ME."

"Yeah," Missy heard herself say, "about that. The thing is, for you to Ride, I have to be on board with it." She pulled herself straighter. "And I'm not."

War's eyes gleamed like rubies. "YOU ARE A TOY DOG YAPPING AT THE FEET OF A WOLF. YIELD NOW, AND I WILL LEAVE YOU INTACT. RUN AWAY, AND LIVE."

Adam's voice, colder than steel: *Run home and cry to your mommy.*

Melissa Miller lifted her chin and told the Red Rider to go to hell.

"OH, GIRL," War said happily. "I'M GOING TO ENJOY THIS VERY, VERY MUCH." And then she lunged at Missy.

‖‖‖‖

A fourth horse now stood with the other three, its coat immaculately white, a nimbus of dust around it like a halo of smog. Pestilence took a seat on the left side of Death, who slid the White Rider a look. "Feeling better?"

"For the moment."

Black, Pale, and White watched the dance of the Red.

After a time, Pestilence commented, "You have a very strange taste in women."

Death smiled, his gaze on the girl at the bottom of the steps. "The struggle of humanity is all 'hot ice and wondrous strange snow'. It is a fascinating contradiction. And War has always embodied it well."

"Your latest embodiment is poised to destroy the world," said Famine.

"Maybe," Death agreed cheerfully. "Isn't it exciting?"

‖‖‖‖

Missy threw herself to the right, barely avoiding War's gauntleted hands. She landed hard on the ground, her face kissing grass. Spitting dirt, she rolled left just as a heavy boot sailed past in a kick that would have taken off her head.

Oh God oh God oh God! She scuttled backward, her heart in her throat as War lumbered after her.

"I AM GOING TO TEAR YOU APART," War crooned, "ONE PIECE AT A TIME."

But first, War would have to catch her. Crab-crawling backward, Missy moved out of kicking range, then scrambled to her feet. She dashed to the far end of the field until she was in the goal box. Beyond the soccer field, there was nothing—no bleachers of seats, no locker room, no trees or buildings or anything. She was trapped.

Panting, she turned to face War, who was closing the distance. If she had the Sword in her hands, she could fight back properly. But War, apparently, *was* the Sword. And she didn't seem inclined to let Missy do anything other than bleed. All in all, Missy preferred War as a voice in her head.

Act instead of react, Death said.

Remembering his words, Missy pushed aside her fear—and that allowed her to think. *Armor's slowing her down.* She leaned forward, knees bent, elbows close to her body. *So just keep away from her, tire her out.*

Did the embodiment of war *get* tired?

War's hands rose overhead as she approached, fingers lacing together to form an enormous metal fist. With a roar, she swung her arms down in a killing blow—and Missy dove to the side, tucking in a roll. She heard War's hands slam into the ground, the impact hard enough to make Missy's teeth rattle.

She was back on her feet as War turned, the red eyes glowing within the shadow of the helm. "STAY STILL, LITTLE GIRL."

Even if someone's coming at you, you can't freeze, Bella said.

And with that memory came an idea. It might have been a bad idea, but Missy was pretty sure her options were limited to Bad Ideas and No Ideas At All. She called out, "Come and get me."

Don't be scared and run away from the ball, Bella coached. *Be confident. Block the shot.*

War lunged forward, her fist cocked back to strike.

I can do it, Missy told herself—a command, a promise, fueled

with the strength of faith. *I can.* She leaned back to let War's
fist sail past—and she caught War's arm, then pivoted down
sharply. War flipped over Missy's shoulder and hit the ground
in a deafening clang of metal.

The sound of steel on steel reverberated, and Missy understood deep in her soul that the Sword was hers, no matter what
its form.

It was *hers.*

And just like that, she knew what to do.

War pulled herself up, planting first one foot and then the
other. She rose to her full height, radiating violence. "I WILL
KILL YOU AND WEAR YOUR SKIN AS MY CLOTHING."

Melissa Miller held out her hand. Words had power, Death
had told her. And so did actions. She threw all her willpower
into one word, knowing it would work because she wielded the
Sword. She opened her mouth and she commanded: "STOP."

And War stopped.

Missy would have smiled, but she was too busy thinking as
hard as she could that War was the Sword, and the Sword was
hers, so therefore she controlled War. Control, just as Death
had been telling her—it had always been about control.

The Red Rider loomed over Missy, frozen in her rage.
Her bellow would have made dragons tremble. *"WHAT ARE
YOU DOING?"*

"Wielding you," Missy said through clenched teeth. "You're
my Sword. You're my tool. That's all you are—just a tool."

War's eyes narrowed, but those hot coals burned no less
brightly. "EVEN THE SMALLEST OF TOOLS MAY KILL THEIR WIELD-
ERS. AND I AM FAR FROM SMALL."

Missy's knees threatened to give out.

Just a tool, Missy told herself. *I wield the Sword. The Sword is a blade. And I've been handling a blade for a long, long time.*

I can do this.

She blew out a shaky breath and ignored the sweat trickling down her face. War's arms shook in her effort to break free, but Missy had bottled her in a glass jar. All she had to do was figure out how to seal it tight, and then she could relax.

But the glass jar broke so easily in the past. Could she ever truly let her guard down and risk War bursting free?

War, like the other Horsemen, must have been able to read Missy's mind, for she declared: "YOU *WILL* TIRE, AND YOUR CONCENTRATION WILL SLIP. AND WHEN IT DOES, I WILL DESTROY YOU. YOU CANNOT LOCK ME AWAY FOREVER, LITTLE GIRL. TRUST ME ON THAT."

Missy felt the familiar pressure in her chest, the slow closing of her throat. Her eyes widened in panic. *Not now! Please, God—I can't lose it now! How do I stop War?*

War's voice, victorious: *TRUST ME ON THAT.*

It hit her in an epiphany, shattering her and rebuilding her all at once: it wasn't about bottling her emotions or fighting them for dominance, or slicing herself when it was all too much. She couldn't control what she didn't trust.

Trust.

She kept her rage within and then cut to let it out. Could she trust herself enough to release her rage without the blade?

Yes, she thought, a smile blooming on her face. Trust. It was stronger than power, subtler than influence. She could simply let herself feel, acknowledge the bad and embrace the good— and between the two, come to an acceptance.

She could learn not to merely survive but to live.

Melissa Miller, sixteen and a self-injurer, looked upon the embodiment of her rage. "I accept you," Missy said, opening her arms wide. "I accept *me.*"

With a savage roar, the Red Rider pounced.

Missy, unafraid, closed her arms around the knight and embraced her, embraced herself as a torrent of emotion flooded her. Violence and hatred and loathing and bitterness and too many other feelings to name hammered her, ravaged her . . . and washed over her without dragging her under. She felt them all, and let them go.

How does one stop war? By offering peace.

|||||

On the bottom steps of the school, a young woman hugged herself. By her feet lay the symbol of War.

Famine glanced at the Pale Rider. "You knew it would end thus?"

"I'm not a fortuneteller," said Death.

"But you knew all the same."

A tiny smile played on Death's lips. "So tell me, wielder of the Scales and blight of abundance. Are we once again in balance?"

Famine stood and looked down at him, her face shrouded by the wide brim of her black hat. "You already know the answer."

Death chuckled softly. "Indeed. Go thee out unto the world, Black Rider. And have a little fun while you're at it."

She touched her gloved hand to her hat. "Gentlemen," she said. And then she and her steed were gone.

||||||

"I HATE YOU," War murmured in Missy's ear.

"That's okay," said Missy, hugging War all the tighter. "I've hated me for a long time. But I'm ready to let that go now."

"I AM THE BEST PART OF YOU," War said, her voice fading.

"Maybe. But you're just a part of me. Nothing more . . ."

The empty armor crashed to the ground.

". . . and nothing less," Missy finished.

||||||

Death glanced at the White Rider. "We Four were together," he said. "And I couldn't help but notice there was no Last Battle."

Pestilence sniffed. "We were together, yes. But we weren't Riding." And then he exited in a sneeze of white.

||||||

Melissa Miller, alone on the battlefield outside of her school, let out a shaky breath. Tears streamed down her face, and her smile was a thing of radiant beauty.

"Well, now," said Death, grinning as he walked down the stairs. "The things we do to get out of class."

Chapter 19

Missy wiped away her tears as she faced the Pale Rider. "She was part of me all along, wasn't she?"

"Once you accepted the Sword? Of course. You think I was calling you War because it was a code name?" Death smiled warmly. "Okay, maybe it would make a good code name. But no, I was calling you by your office, by your title. By your name. Thou art War, Melissa Miller."

She nodded, and she was surprised by how right that sounded. She was War, the Red Rider of the Apocalypse. And she was Missy Miller. "I'm not sure how I'm going to fit in all the warring with classes and stuff."

"You'll figure it out." Death paused, and Missy was once again struck by how incredibly human he seemed, from the way his hair moved in the wind to the slouch of his shoulders—that, and so much more. He said, "You know, the other Horsemen have turned their backs on their human lives. Pestilence did so long ago, and Famine more recently. But they've left that part of themselves behind. You could do the same."

No more pre-calc classes? Now *that* was tempting.

Missy smiled sheepishly and shook her head. "I've just come to terms with a new part of myself. I'm not ready to leave any other pieces right now." Her smile turned rueful. "Besides, I don't have my driver's license yet."

Death laughed, and the sound was sweet to Missy's ears. "There is much that awaits you. And I am pleased that you've fully accepted your charge." He motioned to her, and she looked down at herself to see that her soccer uniform had been replaced with a duster, vest, pants, and boots, all leather, and all a fiery red-orange, like lava. The shirt beneath the vest felt like silk. Only her goalkeeper gloves remained the same.

Missy, momentarily stunned, forgot just how exhausted she was. Grinning like a kid locked in a candy shop, Missy spun around. "Okay, this is seriously cool."

"It is," said Death, stepping up to her, smiling softly, his eyes shining with secrets. "And it's only the beginning." He touched her cheek lightly, a small stroke and then his hand was gone, but that one touch was enough to speed up her heart.

Flushing, she looked up into his blue, blue eyes. "Why me?" she asked softly. "I'm just a girl. No one special. Why did you pick me?"

Something mischievous played along Death's face. "You're assuming I did the picking. And you're asking the wrong question." He took her hands in his, and even through the gloves she felt the chill of his fingers. "The real question is, why *not* you?"

For that, Missy had no answer. So she just looked up into Death's face, and she thought she saw her future written in his gaze.

"A question for a question," he said, still holding her hands. "Why do you believe you killed your cat?"

The words startled her. "She died in my arms."

"Graygirl was fourteen and sick, and you held her as the veterinarian put her to sleep. Why do you believe you killed her?"

Missy blinked away sudden tears. "It was my call," she said, her voice breaking. "Mom and Dad would have let the vet put a tube in her chest to help with her breathing, but they let me make the call because she had always been my cat, from when she was a kitten. I got her when I was two," she said, smiling with the vague memory of an eight-week-old kitten, a ball of gray fuzz, kneading her paws on Missy's lap. "Sure, she was the family cat, but she was mine, you know? She followed me and stayed in my room and slept in my bed. She chose me."

"Yes," said Death.

"And I chose to let her go." Missy's chest tightened . . . but she didn't feel the pressing need to drag a razor across her belly. She was horribly sad, and it felt as if a hand were squeezing her heart. But she didn't want to cut.

"Some would say you gave her a blessing. You sent her on her way to peace."

"Is that what happens after?" Missy asked, peering into his eyes. "Peace?"

"That would be telling," he said, winking.

She let out a laugh, and for the first time since Graygirl died, she didn't feel guilty. She loved her cat and always would. It was time to let the pain go.

"See that?" Death said softly. "Right there, that's the amazing thing about you, about all people. You learn."

He smiled at her, and Missy's sadness melted, leaving her drained but not completely empty—not as long as she had the memory of Graygirl to fill her once again.

Death murmured, "I have to go."

She wanted to tell him to stay, but she knew better. "Will I see you again?"

"Before you know it. War and Death work very . . ." He squeezed her hands, once. ". . . *very* well together."

She had only thought she had blushed before. Now her entire face was on fire.

"Go thee out unto the world, Red Rider," said Death. "Live your life, Melissa Miller. Our paths will cross again."

He released her hands, and she had a wild urge to kiss him before he left.

"When you're ready, I'll be here." He grinned. "I'm a patient sort of personification."

Yes, Death was patient. But War wasn't known for her patience.

Missy wrapped her arms around his neck and stood on her toes as she pulled him down to meet her halfway. She pressed her lips against his and kissed him. And kissed him.

Death's lips, warmed by War's passion, weren't cold at all.

||||||

After the Pale Rider left, Missy patted Ares' neck. "Go home," she told it fondly, "wherever that is for you. We won't be Riding today."

The horse nickered softly.

"I'm fine," she said. "Just tired. Been a long day. Math test, completely mortified by a bunch of idiots, kicked off the soccer team, confronted War, kissed Death." Missy smiled, her lips still tingling from Death's touch. "It's just my third day on the job. Do I get a learning curve?"

The steed seemed to think about it, then it snorted its approval.

"Thanks," she said, rubbing behind its ears. "I'll call you when I'm ready to Ride."

Ares leapt into the sky and disappeared in a wink of fire.

Missy turned to face her school and slowly walked up the stairs. By the time she reached the top, her clothing had shimmered into her black shirt, cutoff shorts, stockings, and sneakers.

With a sigh, Melissa Miller opened the door and stepped back into her life.

EPILOGUE
TWO MONTHS LATER

In stories, the guy gets the girl, Good defeats Evil, and there's always a happily ever after. In real life, you strive for that happy ending, but it doesn't always work out that way. Sometimes, you have to compromise.

Melissa Miller wasn't allowed back on the varsity soccer team that year. She had to put up with daily taunts from Trudy and Jenna, which she managed better some days than others. One time, after Jenna made a particularly nasty comment about Missy's sexual habits, Missy let War out to play—just enough to make her eyes burn and let Jenna feel exactly how angry she made Missy . . . and what Missy could do about it if she so desired—and for the next week, neither Jenna nor Trudy even looked at her. As far as Missy was concerned, that was a blessing.

She was struggling with pre-calc and had been given notice that if her grade didn't improve, she wouldn't be eligible for AP math her senior year.

The two weeks after Kevin's disastrous party, she was still the school laughingstock. And then one of the Matts hit on some girl at the pizzeria . . . except the girl turned out to be a guy. One month later, Matt was still gossip fodder.

Missy hung out with Erica a lot more, and she remembered why they had been friends in the first place. The debate over real-life romance versus air-quotes romance continued, but Missy was starting to come around to Erica's way of thinking.

Missy also started talking to the school guidance counselor. The only reason she did it at first was to prove to her soccer coach that she was serious about getting back on the team next year, but Missy was pleasantly surprised to discover that the guidance counselor wasn't a bad sort. One day, Missy took a leap of faith and told the counselor about her tendency to reach for a razor. Over the next few weeks, the counselor talked with Missy almost every day, and soon she convinced Missy to come clean to her parents.

She did. Her mom cried and her dad was shocked, but they listened to her. Even Sue listened, and when Missy was done talking, Sue actually hugged her. Then she called Missy an idiot. Her mom begged her to tell her if she ever had the urge to cut again, even if her mom was in a meeting with her company CEO. Her dad said the same thing, loudly, and he repeated himself every night for the next month. Her parents were still obscenely busy, and Sue still hung with the popular crowd—some things, after all, would never change. But Missy found it a little easier to breathe when she was home.

Every once in a while, she volunteered at the local teen crisis hot line. Her parents thought she did it for her college applications. Her sister thought she did it as a sort of joke. In truth, Missy didn't know why she did it. But the few times she spoke with other kids who hurt themselves, she was able to help, a little. And that made her feel good.

The family rescued two kittens from the animal shelter. One of them, a russet-colored ball of energy, Missy named Mars. Her sister thought she was talking about the planet.

She saw Adam at school. She ignored him.

She played Nirvana a lot.

Some nights, she climbed atop Ares and soared across the skies, and she helped people release their rage and find a temporary peace. Other nights, her emotions got the better of her, and when she traveled on her warhorse she left turmoil in her wake.

She saw Death and shared stolen moments of intimacy.

Sometimes, she saw the other Horsemen as she went out into the world. Famine didn't quite trust her, and it was a toss-up whether Pestilence was in his right mind. But they accepted her as War.

Not perfect, no. Not a storybook ending. But Missy wasn't complaining.

||||||

Melissa Miller hasn't cut since the day she accepted War within her. The lockbox is still in her closet, buried under her soccer equipment, gone but not forgotten. There may come a time when she once again reaches for the blade within. But every day that goes by that Missy doesn't cut, she considers a victory.

And if there's one thing that motivates War, it's victory.

It took me the better part of ten years before I sat down to write *Hunger,* my first Horseman novel about an anorexic teen who becomes Famine. When I finally wrote it, the words all came pouring out in a matter of weeks. No such luck with *Rage.* I didn't know who the main character would be; I had no idea how the book should end. And the beginning was annoyingly out of reach. I felt utterly lost.

And then my one of my cats died.

Mist was fifteen years old, and sick. We had a choice of putting a chest tube in her or trying steroid treatments to help her breathe. I knew my girl, and a chest tube would have killed her. (When she'd gotten fixed at two years, that started a nervous condition of her picking at her belly. Her fur didn't regrow until she was twelve, when she had mellowed a little.) So we opted for the shot, and for a week, it was better.

And then it wasn't. She was in pain, and unable to move well. She'd stopped eating and barely drank. So we did what we felt was best for her. The boys got a chance to say goodbye to her, and then my husband and I took her to the vet. She sat in my lap, wrapped in a blanket, as the vet gave her a final shot. She let out one final meow—maybe it was a goodbye—and then she died.

It took me a week before I could bear to put away her carrier. As I slid the container onto the shelf, a line came to me:

The day Melissa Miller killed her cat, she saw the Angel of Death. But he was no angel—and he wasn't there for the cat.

And like that, I had my beginning.

As I wrote the prologue, I started researching self-injury. (Unlike with eating disorders, I had no personal experience with cutting.) Along the way, I found a terrific website. *Secret Shame* has a lot of information about self-injury—what it is, and what it's not. Without the candid information posted there, I doubt I could have written *Rage*. I am grateful to Deb Martinson for the site (www.palace.net/llama/psych/injury.html).

Missy slowly revealed herself to me. And I do mean slowly. At first, she was rather timid—and you'd probably agree if you'd read the first draft of the prologue. But as I grew more comfortable writing her story, Missy became bolder. Angrier. And more passionate. It took a while, but I finally *got* her.

It wasn't until after Missy's confrontation with her soccer coach, and its result, that I finally got a bead on the other major character in the book: War. I was about to write what wound up being Chapter 18 when I heard a voice whisper to me, one that was completely unlike anything else I'd heard for this book. It said:

The world is a wound and I will cauterize it.

And I was like, *AAAAAAAAAAAAH*. That's the first time I heard the voice of War. The small caps came later.

(By now, you may be thinking that I'm insane—hearing voices and lines of dialogue and text in my head and whatnot.

Maybe I am a little crazy. But yeah, that's what happens sometimes when I write.)

With War's voice finally clear, I went back and altered some of the earlier dialogue between War and Missy. And then I wrote the rest of the book. I didn't know how it was going to end until I actually ended it. Sort of cool. And, if you're a control-freak author like me, a little scary. But it was the right ending.

Rage, like *Hunger*, doesn't end easily. There's a reason the last paragraph is in the present tense. Not an easy ending, no. But, I hope, an honest one. Missy still struggles to keep control.

I'm rooting for her.

〢〢〢〢〢

A portion of proceeds for *Rage* will be donated to To Write Love On Her Arms, a nonprofit organization dedicated to presenting hope and finding help for people struggling with self-injury, depression, addiction, and suicide. TWLOHA also invests directly in treatment and recovery. For more information about the organization, please visit the TWLOHA website: **www.twloha.com.** If you bought this book, thank you for helping make a difference.